SALEM BURNING

DANIEL SUGAR

FOR MY MOTHER

The heart is deceitful above all things, and
desperately wicked.

Jeremiah

No exorciser harm thee!
Nor no witchcraft charm thee!

Cymbeline

PROLOGUE

THE LATE-AFTERNOON sun was slipping away and storm clouds and darkness were rapidly approaching as the happy eight-year-old girl carrying a straw basket filled with freshly-cut roses ran towards Delaney Castle.

Suddenly out of breath, Sarah Delaney stopped, sat down on the soft green grass and looked at her home. Delaney Castle was truly beautiful. Its stone walls and turrets so white they almost shimmered in the rapidly setting sun. It was hard to believe that a magnificent castle perched on top of a hill was actually her home. Hers! How lucky she was to live there and how blessed she was to have such wonderful parents. Parents who loved her so much they were making a magnificent birthday party for her that very evening. Overcome with happiness, Sarah could not help herself and as she stood up and ran into the castle she started to sing. "The birth day is the loveliest day. The birth day is filled with charm."

Sarah's beautiful, dark-haired mother, Evelyn Delaney, was clad in a breathtaking saffron gown and she was waiting for her daughter as Sarah ran into the castle.

1

Evelyn smiled, lifted a rose from Sarah's straw basket and inhaled the flower's scent. "Come along, Sarah. Everyone wants to see the birthday girl."

Sarah kissed her mother on the cheek and said, "I am ready, mother."

Sarah took her mother's hand and together they walked into an enormous dining hall which was filled with relatives and friends who began to clap and cheer the moment Sarah entered the room.

Sarah scanned the room. The crowd was thick. There were so many people, too many people - but she only wanted one of them. Yet she could not find him. It was so frustrating. Where was he? Where was he? Suddenly she spotted him - her tall, handsome, blond father, Patrick Delaney, (clad in his finest tartan kilt and a velvet jacket). Sarah rushed into her father's arms and he laughed and tossed her playfully into the air as Sarah squealed with delight. "Now we eat!" Patrick yelled. "Now we sing and dance as we let it be known to all that eight years ago, on the first of June, fifteen hundred and forty-two, my daughter, this young beauty named Sarah Delaney, was born in Scotland!"

The assembled guests cheered and, as if by magic, servants suddenly appeared in the vast dining hall, some carrying trays of food, some holding musical instruments which they began to play.

Delighted, the guests began to eat and sing and dance to the lively music which was almost drowned out by the sound of approaching thunder.

Sarah took her parents' hands and the three of them sang along with their guests; raising their voices as the sounds of distant thunder grew closer and louder.

Suddenly, thunder exploded overhead, cold, impenetrable sheets of rain dropped from the black sky and long branches of lightning illuminated the castle as soldiers rushed into the dining hall with swords drawn.

Sarah Delaney screamed as a soldier cut off her father's head.

Evelyn Delaney grabbed her terrified daughter and ran to the large portrait of Patrick Delaney that hung on one of the dining hall's stone walls.

Soldiers ignored all cries for mercy and massacred the party guests, savagely, brutally, sparing no one.

Trembling, Evelyn pushed the portrait and the stone wall moved, revealing a secret passageway.

Evelyn quickly kissed her daughter. "Hurry now, Sarah. Save yourself."

Suddenly, a soldier drove his sword into Evelyn's chest and Sarah, still clutching the basket of roses rushed down the dark stone passageway.

"Run, Sarah!"

The soldier pulled the sword from Evelyn's chest and then plunged it into her throat.

The moment Evelyn Delaney fell to the ground, dead, the soldier turned his attention to Sarah and rushed into the stone passageway.

As Sarah ran, she turned and looked behind her. The soldier was too fast. She was running with all her might but the soldier was getting closer.

A bright white flash of lightning illuminated the end of the passageway; illuminated freedom.

Sarah, exhausted, managed to squeeze through the passageway's narrow opening just as the soldier lunged and tried to grab her.

The soldier was able to grab Sarah's left shoe and tear if off her foot but Sarah was suddenly free.

The soldier was unable to fit through the passageway's narrow opening and he screamed and swore and waved the child's raw leather shoe as Sarah Delaney ran and ran and disappeared into the wet Scottish night.

1.

AFTERNOON HEAT WAS BAKING Salem as tall, humorless, bespectacled, sixty-year-old doctor Samuel Edwards stood over a small wooden bed and examined six-year-old Nancy Kelley while her young parents June and Harrison silently observed.

In the heat of summer, young Nancy was cold, trembling with fever.

Doctor Edwards handed June Kelley a towel.

June poured water over the towel and handed it back to Doctor Edwards who then placed it on Nancy's neck.

In a small, frightened voice June Kelley said, "She will survive?'"

Doctor Edwards said nothing. He continued to press the wet towel against Nancy's neck.

Harrison Kelley pressed the matter. "Doctor?"

Doctor Edwards did not look Harrison in the eye. "I can promise nothing, Harrison. This plague that has gripped Salem has a mind of its own."

June Kelley began to cry.

Doctor Edwards lit a lantern and then held it up to Nancy's face. A tiny red spot was just visible on the child's left cheek.

June, still crying, held on to her husband.

Doctor Edwards left the Kelley's house and then nailed a small wooden sign to the front door which read: POX.

2.

THE MID-DAY CROWD that had gathered at the top of Gallows Hill watched and listened intently as Judge Henry Stong finished reading a proclamation. "…And so, for your crime of theft, you will, on this third day of June, sixteen hundred and ninety-two, be suspended by the neck until dead, Fisher Cooper. Your body will then be taken from our village of Salem and buried beyond the swamp in Slaves' Cemetery. Have you last words?"

Fisher Cooper, an old, African American slave who was standing on a scaffold, began to tremble as a noose was slipped over his neck. "Please. My wife is sick. So weak. That is why I took the food. Please. Do not do it."

The crowd began to swell as sweaty men, women and children in dusty, dirty, doublets, breeches, gowns, smocks and petticoats, slowly trudged up to the top of Gallows Hill in the hot summer sun carrying cats, dogs, crude toys and picnic baskets.

Judge Stong placed a black hood over Fisher's head.

A drunken, pot-bellied man jumped onto the scaffold. "Take off the hood, Judge. Let us see his thievin' eyes bulge!"

The crowd erupted, screaming and applauding wildly.

Judge Stong surveyed the bloodthirsty crowd, realized he had a potential riot on his hands and, then, reluctantly, removed Fisher's hood. "God rest you, Fisher Cooper."

Fisher, terrified, tried to speak but could not.

Judge Stong motioned to the executioner whose hand tightened on a lever.

Happy, screaming children chased each other around the scaffold and the crowd cheered as Fisher Cooper's neck snapped.

The drunken, pot-bellied man laughed. "His thievin' legs is twitchin' like a caught fish."

3.

LILLY PARRIS, A PLAIN, eighteen-year-old teenage girl clad in a simple white dress and white bonnet, walked into Bay Church and sat in a box pew facing the pulpit. Candles, scattered throughout the large, hot, empty wooden church flickered as Lilly, clutching her crucifix, prayed. "Help me, Father. I will change. I promise I will. I want your love. Show me your love."

Lilly knelt, shut her eyes and pressed her crucifix to her breast.

Suddenly, Lilly heard screams from the top of Gallows Hill and, frightened, moved toward a window. Lilly understood what had happened and she sadly said one word, "Fisher."

Lilly left the church and walked through fields of summer flowers, past oxen pulling stumps, women winnowing grain and men shearing sheep. When she reached a cedar rail fence enclosing an apple orchard, Lilly hopped the fence and walked toward a small, crumbling, wooden shack.

Susan Cooper, a beautiful, nineteen-year-old African American teenage girl in a ragged dress, ran from the shack towards Lilly. "Oh, Miss Parris, I have lost 'em both now."

Lilly hugged the young woman. "Susan, be strong. For your mother."

Susan opened her mouth to say something and then fainted.

Lilly knelt down, kissed Susan on the cheek, and then moved, slowly, toward the shack. The door opened easily and Lilly moved inside, blind suddenly, in the hot, cramped darkness. Slowly, her eyes adjusted and she saw Susan's mother, Leonora Cooper, hanging from a wooden beam. "Merciful God," said Lilly.

• • •

That evening, a thick, yellow, ground-level mist that smelled of sulfur rolled into Slaves' Cemetery from the nearby swamp. The unkempt cemetery was filled with cheap, crude headstones. Weeds were everywhere and unburied African American children, covered in horrifying smallpox lesions, were rotting in piles on the cemetery's soggy ground.

With great effort, Lilly and Susan carefully lowered the bodies of Leonora and Fisher Cooper into freshly-dug graves.

As Lilly began to shovel dirt onto the bodies she said, "They are together now. At peace."

Susan picked up a shovel and looked at Lilly. "And we will find 'em a nice marker stone?"

"The most beautiful one you have ever seen. You will do them proud."

As Susan started to softly cry, Lilly put her arm around Susan, kissed her cheek and stroked her hair. "It is going to be fine, Susan."

"There is nothin' for me here. My brother was sold to Boston. Maybe I can get there."

"Nonsense. Grandmother Rose needs some help. You will work for her. There is a small cottage in back. Plenty of room."

Susan hugged Lilly tightly. "I know it ain't allowed, Miss Parris, but you are a good friend to the slaves."

Lilly kissed Susan again. "You know I have always loved you, Susan."

As Lilly and Susan continued to shovel dirt into the graves a coral snake with red and black markings slithered towards Susan's leg.

Lilly stopped shoveling and calmly turned toward Susan. "Do not move, Susan. There is a snake about six inches from your left leg."

Startled, Susan quickly shook her left leg and yelled, "Get away!"

The coral snake struck, biting Susan's left leg.

Susan screamed as Lilly quickly killed the snake with a shovel.

Susan slumped to the ground, rubbing the fresh puncture marks on her leg. "I will be joinin' 'em in the grave tonight."

Lilly carefully examined the dead snake, stroking its colorful skin. "No, look, you are fine, see?"

Susan, terrified, kept rubbing the puncture marks on her leg and did not look up. "I am bit. I am dead."

"Do you not know the rhyme?"

"Do not go tellin' me no rhymes, girl. I am dyin'."

Lilly, still holding the dead snake, sat down next to Susan. "The skin is black and red, see? 'If red touches yellow, you are a dead fellow. If red touches black, you are okay, Jack.' It is not poisonous. You will just be bruised and sore."

Lilly stood up, moved into the bushes and began to gather berries. Once she had collected a handful, she sat down next to Susan and crushed the berries into the wound.

Susan gasped and then smiled. "The pain is goin' away."

"Nothing like Dewberry for a snake bite."

Susan smiled. "You know nature's secrets."

Lilly said to her friend, "It is time to get you home."

4.

GRANDMOTHER ROSE'S LARGE HOUSE was lovely and comfortable. Three stories with four bedrooms, a large kitchen, a dining room, a big beautiful sitting room, a welcoming front parlor and six well-crafted stone fireplaces.

When Lilly and Susan entered the house, (Susan limping with an arm around Lilly's shoulder for support), they found Grandmother Rose, (an old, elegant woman whose hair was, still, surprisingly dark), sitting in the dining room stitching a quilt with her friends: the white-haired Mrs. Black and Widow Wheeler, (who walked with a slight limp and the aid of a cane and who always wore a pretty, frilly, cotton cap in order to hide her baldness).

"Oh, that leg. She is limping terribly!" Grandmother Rose almost shouted as a grandfather clock began to softly chime.

Lilly said, "She will be fine, Grandmother Rose. It was a coral."

"It is ten o'clock," said Widow Wheeler. "We were just about to have tea and cakes. You will both join us."

"Yes. You must," Mrs. Black insisted.

Grandmother Rose left her two friends, stood up and went to Susan. "Now, put your other arm around my shoulder, dear, and we will both help you get upstairs."

Susan did as she was told and reluctantly let Lilly and Grandmother Rose help her up the stairs.

"Excuse me, Mrs. Black, Widow Wheeler. We will just be upstairs a moment," said Grandmother Rose.

"You just holler if you need more help, Grandmother Rose and we will come on up," Widow Wheeler replied.

Grandmother Rose, Lilly and Susan moved slowly through the elegant home. Past the large kitchen, up the stairs and into a well-appointed bedroom. When they finally reached the bedroom, Susan practically collapsed onto the canopy bed and almost immediately began to drift off to sleep.

Quietly, Lilly said, "They are both gone, Grandmother Rose."

"I know dear, it is an awful thing."

"I told her -"

"Of course. Susan will stay here. She is asleep already. Let her rest now and I will talk to her in the morning."

"I am going to church."

"Fine. But first the two of us will have a talk."

Grandmother Rose and Lilly walked downstairs and then went outside to Grandmother Rose's herb garden. The garden was large and colorful; filled with a wide assortment of plants, flowers and herbs including hemlock, foxglove, juniper, pimpernel, marjoram, wallflower, marigold, meadowsweet and mint.

Lilly popped a mint leaf into her mouth and began to chew. "The most beautiful garden in all of Salem."

Grandmother Rose smiled. "It is a lovely spot. A beautiful place for an engagement party."

Lilly frowned. "Do not start that again."

Grandmother Rose said, "I promised your parents I would see you married. How can I when you never make an effort? So many eligible young men in this village and you spend all your time locked up in that church."

"Oh, Grandmother Rose, it is no use. We both know I am plain. No boy is going to waste his breath on me."

"Lilly, you have given up without even trying. There is much you do not know about young men. You will be surprised at how they will take to you."

"You are so sweet to me, Grandmother Rose but my looking glass does not lie. I know boys do not want me."

Grandmother Rose removed the white bonnet from Lilly's head, freeing long, thick, dark hair. "Would you do an old woman a favor? Make me a promise?"

"You know I cannot refuse you."

"There is a social at Town Hall next week."

"Not that. It is too humiliating. No one will dance with me."

"Do it for your old grandmother."

"I will do it but now I really must go." Lilly kissed Grandmother Rose on the cheek and then walked away.

"There are no answers in that empty church, Lilly."

Lilly did not answer her grandmother, and, as she continued to walk away, as she was enveloped by the warm, soundless night, Grandmother Rose shouted into the darkness, "God cannot help you. We are what we are, Lilly!"

5.

As LILLY QUICKLY WALKED toward Bay Church she approached the gristmill and when she reached it she stopped, (as she always did), sat down on the wooden fence surrounding the gristmill and tossed pebbles at the mill's huge, overshot waterwheel.

Lilly was about to leave the gristmill and continue on her way when she heard the sound of horses approaching. She quickly turned her head and discovered a riding party rapidly approaching. There were four men on horseback, all carrying torches: handsome, blond Kyle Edwards, Kyle's father, Doctor Samuel Edwards, gunsmith Charles Mackenzie and boot maker Daniel Flynn.

Kyle pulled on his horse's reins and came to a stop right in front of Lilly.

Lilly frowned as she looked at Kyle and remembered how cruel he and his friends had been to her when she was a little girl. She remembered an awful day when she was just nine years old and she was leaving Bay Church and Kyle and his friends were laughing at her and pointing at the ground. Pointing at a picture they had drawn in the dirt with sticks. A terrible, ugly, picture of her and the words they had carved into the dirt: SPINSTER LILLY PARRIS. They had all run away, of course. All laughing. They were terrible cowards. And she had sat on the ground and bravely erased the terrible picture and the terrible words; her hands covered with dirt and her cheeks covered with tears.

Kyle Edwards was the last person Lilly wanted to see but she had been raised to be polite and so she smiled benignly.

"Lilly Parris. What is a young girl doing out alone this time of evening?" Kyle demanded.

Lilly's eyes narrowed. How dare he question her? "I am not young, Kyle Edwards. We are the same age. In fact, I am three days older. So why are you out at this hour, young man?"

Daniel Flynn, Samuel Edwards and Charles Mackenzie laughed.

"Let us hope the new sights I have designed for these guns are as sharp as your tongue, my girl," said Charles Mackenzie.

Lilly hopped off the wooden fence and then patted the head of Kyle's horse.

"Careful," said Kyle. "He kicks."

"He won't kick me. What are you hunting?" asked Lilly.

Once again, Daniel, Samuel and Charles laughed.

Doctor Edwards said, "We are wanting white-tail deer, brave child. And where are you heading?"

"To church. But I would rather hunt deer. Take me with you."

Daniel Flynn laughed and looked at Doctor Edwards. "Can you imagine it, Doctor? Hunting with a girl? Think of it!"

Lilly hopped onto Kyle's horse and grabbed the gun that was slung, on a strap, over Kyle's head. "I can hunt. I killed a coral a few hours ago."

Kyle was outraged. "Get her off my horse, father. I would like to get to those deer before sunrise."

Doctor Edwards laughed and whipped his horse violently with a crop. As his horse began to move, the doctor looked back at his son. "Do it yourself, my son. We are off."

Charles and Daniel whipped their horses and followed the doctor.

Kyle was furious. He turned and looked Lilly straight in the eye. "I want you off this horse now, Lilly Parris!"

Lilly laughed. "Afraid your friends will learn that a girl beat you at the hunt?"

Kyle quickly said, "Neither I, nor my friends, think of you as a girl."

"I hate you, Kyle Edwards. The girls are all wrong. You are not handsome. Beneath that handsome mask is ugliness."

"You have three seconds to get off this horse, Lilly Parris. I will not miss this hunt because of you."

"Then I suggest we move on."

Lilly grabbed Kyle's riding crop, whipped the horse and together they rode off to join the hunt.

• • •

Within ten minutes, Kyle and Lilly had caught up with Doctor Edwards, Daniel Flynn and Charles Mackenzie and, as they approached the hunting party, Kyle shouted, "Any luck, father?"

Doctor Edwards laughed. "About as much as you have had, son. Glad you could join us, Lilly."

"We have heard some rustling in the woods," said Daniel Flynn. "But we have had no luck spotting deer. The damn moon keeps going behind the clouds. Even with our torches, the night is too black."

Lilly sensed something and her eyes narrowed. "We must go back. We are in danger."

Charles Mackenzie scoffed, "You are a scared, silly girl."

Lilly would not back down. She raised her voice. "Please believe me."

Charles Mackenzie could not hide his disgust. "Shut up, girl! We stay and hunt. Speak again and you will walk the miles home."

The hunting party's torches were barely flickering now. And suddenly, hot summer thunder shattered the still of the night and lightning illuminated the sky and a hard rain extinguished the flickering torches just as the wolves that had been tracking the hunting party leapt from their hiding places in the woods.

Doctor Edwards shouted, "Wolves! The guns!"

The men scrambled for their weapons as three wolves sank their teeth into Charles Mackenzie's horse and the frightened, wounded animal lost its balance and fell to the slippery, muddy ground.

Charles Mackenzie screamed and screamed as the wolves leapt on him and ate him alive.

Lilly, still holding Kyle's gun, shot a wolf that was running towards Doctor Edwards. The wolf was killed instantly.

19

Doctor Edwards raised his gun and fired. Another wolf fell over dead.

Lilly fired again. Another kill. Then another.

A wolf leapt through the air towards Daniel Flynn. Flynn screamed, "To hell with you!" and pounded the animal with the butt of his gun, smashing its skull.

The four survivors looked at each other. All seemed calm when suddenly a wolf leapt from the bushes and sank its teeth into Kyle Edwards' horse and then into Kyle's Edwards' right arm.

Kyle's horse collapsed as Kyle screamed.

Calmly, Lilly narrowed her eyes, aimed and then shot the wolf between the eyes.

The animal collapsed; its teeth still buried deep in Kyle's arm.

Doctor Edwards pried the dead wolf's jaws open, drawing the teeth from Kyle's arm as Lilly cradled Kyle's head and stroked his wet blond hair.

Kyle, barely conscious, moaned.

"Tree sap will seal that wound, doctor, said Lilly."

"Do not be ridiculous, girl. I will get him home to my surgery. My son needs treatment not the recipes of old wives," Doctor Edwards condescended.

Doctor Edwards and Daniel Flynn placed Kyle onto one of the two horses that survived the wolf attack. Doctor Edwards then got onto the horse with Kyle.

Daniel Flynn picked up Charles Mackenzie's dead body and then mounted the other horse. "Well, come along, girl," Daniel said to Lilly.

"I will make my own way home," said Lilly.

"There is danger here, Lilly," said Doctor Edwards.

"The danger is past. Please, just get Kyle home. He needs treatment."

"There are Indians," said, Daniel Flynn.

Lilly laughed. "There are no Indians. And I would not care if there were. They are good folk."

Doctor Edwards said, "You are being very foolish, girl."

Lilly sighed. "Please, just go. I prefer to walk."

Doctor Edwards was Salem's only physician. He was trusted and respected. He was used to giving orders and having those orders immediately obeyed. He was certainly not about to argue with a girl. And so, Doctor Edwards said, dismissively, "As you like."

The men rode off, leaving Lilly alone in the forest.

Lilly began to hum softly to herself. She lifted her arms above her head and started to spin, dancing and singing in the warm, wet, humid forest. Finally, exhausted, she dropped down onto the wet ground in order to catch her breath.

As her breathing returned to normal, Lilly's gaze fell upon the dead wolf that had bitten Kyle. The jaws of the wolf were still open - white, bloody teeth gleaming in the darkness.

Lilly picked up a large stone, moved to the dead wolf and then used the large stone to smash a tooth from the animal's mouth. She then put the tooth into the pocket of her dress and started the long walk home.

6.

WHILE LILLY WALKED HOME through the woods, six-year-old Nancy Kelley clutched her doll and slept as June Kelley held a candle up to her daughter's innocent face and discovered that the tiny red spot on Nancy's left cheek had grown larger.

Terrified and overcome with sadness, June Kelley sat down on the rocking chair next to her sleeping daughter's bed, blew out the candle and started to cry.

7.

Very early the next morning, Doctor Edwards' wife, Mary, an extremely pretty woman with long blonde hair, was already awake and already stirring a stew which cooked in a large, central fireplace.

Doctor Edwards, smoking a pipe, was pacing. "The bite is festering, Mary. Kyle's body is filled with poison."

"You are a wonderful doctor, Samuel." Mary filled a bowl with hot stew. "I will take this up to Kyle now. He will need his strength."

Mary walked upstairs to Kyle's bedroom. Kyle was lying on the bed naked, his body bathed in the early morning light. Kyle's body was covered with sweat and his teeth were chattering. "Kyle, it is time to try some food, son."

Kyle did not respond to his mother. He was delirious from the fever, from the poison spreading through his bloodstream. His mother was nothing more than a blur to him; a shape that was making unintelligible sounds. Kyle ignored the shape and the noise and muttered gibberish to himself.

Mary sat on the bed and attempted to feed Kyle a spoonful of stew. The attempt was in vain - the stew just dribbled down the side of Kyle's mouth.

Mary, crying, moved toward the bedroom door just as Doctor Edwards entered the bedroom carrying a glass jar.

"I will pull the poison out of him, Mary." Doctor Edwards examined Kyle's wounded right arm - it was infected, festering. Green pus oozed from the wolf bite.

Doctor Edwards reached into the glass jar and pulled out a handful of leeches which he applied to Kyle's wound.

Kyle screamed.

8.

ONE HOUR LATER, a fire burned brightly in a pit that had been dug in the center of Grandmother Rose's herb garden, and Susan Cooper boiled water in a black pot that sat on the lively fire.

Lilly, moved, slowly, through the garden and gathered herbs which she placed into a large wooden bowl. "Thank you for starting the fire, Susan. I will be fine now."

"Should I stay a while? Maybe you will be needin' me."

"I am fine. You go inside and help Grandmother Rose prepare lunch."

Susan ran into the house and left Lilly alone in the garden.

Lilly continued to collect herbs until she came to a purple plant which caused her to hesitate. Lilly reached for the plant but then stopped and looked around the garden to be absolutely certain she was alone. Satisfied, she quickly picked the purple plant and tossed it into the bowl with the rest of the herbs. She then emptied the contents of the wooden bowl into the boiling water and stirred the concoction with a long wooden stick. The fire hissed and popped as the herbs danced in the boiling water. Lilly's eyes narrowed as she pulled the broken, bloody wolf's tooth from the pocket of her dress and tossed it into the boiling water. "Poison fights poison," Lilly said as she continued to stir the herbs, unaware that Grandmother Rose was watching from a bedroom window.

9.

GRANDMOTHER ROSE WATCHED with great interest as Lilly moved through the garden collecting herbs. She hated how alone her granddaughter was. She hated the fact that Lilly spent most of her life kneeling and praying in Bay Church. Grandmother Rose knew that prayer was not the answer for Lilly, knew that being alone in an empty wooden church would not, ultimately, give Lilly any peace or security. She wanted her beloved granddaughter to have love, to have a husband and children. She wanted Lilly to have a family. And friends. Grandmother Rose wanted to go to Lilly and tell her everything; all the hopes and dreams, all the wonderful things she wished for her granddaughter, all the happiness she wanted her to have but instead Grandmother Rose stood, silently, in the bedroom window and watched as Lilly collected herbs.

10.

JUNE KELLEY GREETED DOCTOR EDWARDS with a cup of tea as he made his way into the Kelley's house. "Thank you for coming so quickly, doctor. I know your own son is not well. Have you had your lunch?"

"I have eaten, thank you," Doctor Edwards said, all business, as he ignored the offered tea and quickly made his way to Nancy Kelley's bedroom.

Nancy, still sleeping, was still holding her doll.

Doctor Edwards gently turned the sleeping child's head and discovered the red spot had metastasized all the way to Nancy's left eye. The large red mark seemed to move, to grow, right before the doctor's eyes.

Frustrated and exhausted, Doctor Edwards shut his eyes and rubbed his temples.

11.

EARLY THAT EVENING, Kyle Edwards was still lying on his bed, naked. His breathing was shallow and his infected right arm twitched continuously.

Mary and Samuel Edwards stood next to Kyle's bed.

Doctor Edwards placed a bible on Kyle's chest. "He will not see the morning, Mary."

"Could you try more leeches?" Mary asked hopefully.

"It is a lost cause. I have failed again. First the children of Salem and now our own son. I saw pretty little Nancy Kelley again this afternoon. The pox has its teeth in her, poor child. I tell you, Mary, our town has fallen under a black curse and I am powerless to stop it."

"You are a wonderful doctor, Samuel. Kyle's accident was not your fault. Nor was this plague; this pox that has gripped the children of Salem. God is testing you, Samuel. But you will find the answer. I know you will. Now please, I beg you, sleep a while. You look haggard."

Doctor Edwards took his wife's hand and, together, they left Kyle's bedroom.

• • •

Later that night, as Samuel and Mary Edwards slept, Lilly Parris, carrying a small glass jar filled with thick, dark, paste, climbed through Kyle Edwards' open bedroom window. "If all the girls who think you are the best-looking young man in Salem could see you right now, Kyle Edwards, they would not be so impressed, would they?"

Kyle opened his eyes and tried to focus but Lilly was just a blur in her simple white dress and bonnet. The young man then tried to speak but merely muttered something incomprehensible.

"Shut your eyes and sleep, Kyle. You will be fine soon enough. Sleep."

Kyle shut his eyes.

Lilly positioned the glass jar over Kyle's right arm and then tipped the jar and poured a thick black paste onto Kyle's infected wound. She then took a piece of white cotton from the pocket of her dress and carefully wrapped the wound. Finally, Lilly opened Kyle's mouth and, using her finger, swabbed Kyle's tongue, gums and cheeks with the black paste.

Kyle, half-asleep, gagged on the foul-tasting paste.

"I know - it is awful. But it is just a bad dream. When you wake up it will all be over."

Kyle shuddered but he swallowed the bitter herbal paste as Lilly continued to feed it to him.

Finally, the glass jar of herbal paste was empty and Lilly said, "Now, a long, deep sleep, Kyle. Fight the fever tonight."

Lilly climbed back through the open bedroom window and shut it behind her as the kerosene lamps in Kyle's bedroom began to die.

• • •

Twenty minutes later, Lilly Parris was facing the pulpit; kneeling and praying in Bay Church. "I have sinned, Father. Please. Understand. I am so alone."

12.

LILLY, GRANDMOTHER ROSE and Susan woke up early the next morning so they could bake fruit pies for the upcoming town social.

Grandmother Rose wiped her glistening brow as she kneaded dough. "I promised Widow Wheeler ten pies for the annual Salem summer social. Where am I going to get the energy? This is going to take all day."

Lilly smiled as she too kneaded dough. "That is what you get for your generosity."

Susan, who was peeling apples, said, "My mama always says it is -" Susan stopped mid-sentence, suddenly realizing.

Grandmother Rose put a hand on Susan's shoulder. "It is alright, Susan, tell us what your mother says."

Susan hesitated and then said, "My mama says it ain't no use doin' too much for folks 'cause they won't never 'preciate it anyway."

Grandmother Rose smiled. "She was a wise woman, your mother."

A sudden pounding on the front door startled the three women.

Grandmother Rose left the kitchen and slowly walked to the front door as she said, "Who could that be so early in the morning?" The pounding on the front door continued and Grandmother Rose yelled, "Hold that racket! Wait. Wait."

Grandmother Rose opened the front door and discovered Doctor Edwards looking rumpled and exhausted.

The doctor took off his glasses and rubbed his tired eyes. "Good morning, Grandmother Rose. Is Lilly home?"

"Of course she is home, doctor. We are all home. Do you know what time it is?"

"Grandmother Rose, I apologize for the early hour."

"Well come in then. You look a mess, doctor. Like you slept in your clothes. Go upstairs and wash your face and then I will give you tea and food."

Doctor Edwards walked into the house and then climbed the stairs.

Grandmother Rose returned to the kitchen and said to Lilly, "You have a visitor."

Lilly was not surprised. "I know."

• • •

Ten minutes later, Doctor Edwards and Grandmother Rose were seated at a small wooden table in the herb garden, and Susan was serving them apple juice and tea and bread and jam while Lilly, standing nearby, chewing on a mint leaf, looked on.

Doctor Edwards took a sip of juice and then said, "A miracle has happened, Lilly."

Lilly took the mint leaf out of her mouth. "I go to church three times a day and I have never seen a miracle."

Doctor Edwards drained his glass of juice. "Kyle should have died, Lilly. But he is up and well. He is riding a horse as we speak. And he has been ravenous. My wife can barely keep up with the cooking."

Lilly joined Doctor Edwards and Grandmother Rose at the table. "I am pleased, of course, but why are you telling me this, doctor?"

"Kyle spoke of a strange dream. He said you came to him. He swears you saved his life."

Lilly frowned. "Delirium."

Doctor Edwards smiled. "Obviously. But he wants to see you, Lilly. He asked me to come and apologize for things that may have been said, or done, in jest. Childish pranks. He fears you will not see him. I have never seen him this way. Please. Promise me you will meet with my son."

Lilly put the mint leaf back in her mouth and continued to chew.

13.

AT DUSK, LILLY AND KYLE stood at the edge of a dock and watched a ship as it sailed away from the port of Salem and slowly disappeared.

Lilly smiled. "I love watching the ships drift away. Are they not beautiful?"

"They truly are majestic," Kyle said. "I have often thought of leaving Salem for a life on the sea."

"When will you leave?" Lilly asked calmly, showing no emotion.

"I saw you in my bedroom, Lilly. I was lying half-dead and naked and you were there."

Lilly turned and walked along the dock, away from Kyle. "You are being ridiculous, Kyle Edwards. You had a fever dream."

Kyle followed Lilly. "You saved my life."

"I am not a doctor. Your father saved you. You are talking nonsense."

Kyle reached out, held Lilly's hand and looked her straight in the eye. "I would like to know you, Lilly."

Lilly pulled her hand away. "Do not waste your time with a plain girl, Kyle. The beautiful girls of Salem are eager to do your bidding."

"Please."

"You are acting out of gratitude. You feel you owe me something. You are mistaken. You owe me nothing. Now go back to your life, Kyle Edwards and I will return to mine."

Kyle nodded but said, "We are not done, Lilly Parris."

14.

AT NOON THE NEXT DAY, Main Street was crowded with Salemites, buying and selling, greeting and gossiping. Lilly and Susan, both carrying straw baskets filled with purchases, slowly moved along the street, through the town of Salem.

The young women passed stores and homes, some of which were adorned with small signs that read: POX. Two large men carried a dead child wrapped in a white sheet from one such home.

Lilly and Susan joined a small crowd and watched for a few moments as the child was carried away. When she could no longer bear it, Lilly took Susan's hand and led her away from the sadness.

Eventually, the girls reached a store whose sign read: MARKS' HARNESS SPECIALIZING IN COLLARS, SADDLES, LEATHER.

Lilly said, "Grandmother Rose asked me to check whether the horse harness has been repaired yet."

Lilly and Susan entered the harness shop.

The shop's owner, Tom Marks, (an extremely short, shriveled, almost gnomish man), was bent over a wooden cradle, cooing baby talk at a laughing infant.

Lilly smiled. "Hello, Mr. Marks. And who do we have here?"

"Afternoon, Lilly. I do not believe you have met my beautiful new grandson. His parents left him here to visit today. Come and have a peek."

Lilly hesitated. "We have errands for Grandmother Rose. I really should just pick up the horse harness."

"I am afraid it is not quite done, Lilly. The crown piece and blinker are good as new but I am still working on the throatlatch and bellyband."

Lilly turned and headed for the door. "Thank you, Mister Marks."

Tom Marks rushed after Lilly.

"Wait, Lilly. Do not leave! You forgot to meet my grandson. Come now, hold him just a minute, girl. Your errands will keep."

Tom put his shriveled hand on Lilly's arm and pulled her to the wooden cradle.

Susan followed.

Laughing, Tom Marks reached into the cradle and picked up the baby. "There now, is he not precious? Hold him close and tight now, Lilly. He likes to have his back patted." Tom carefully placed the baby in Lilly's arms. "Rock on your heels, Lilly. It is soothing to the boy."

Lilly tried to focus on Susan and Tom Marks but they began to fade away and the room started to spin.

Lilly screamed and covered her eyes with her hands, allowing the baby to fall.

In a flash, Susan dropped to the ground, catching the infant before it hit the hardwood floor.

"My God!" shouted Tom Marks.

Tom Marks grabbed the screaming, frightened infant from Susan. "Are you insane? You almost killed him. Get out!"

Lilly staggered from the shop and doubled over in pain.

Susan, terrified, put her arm around Lilly. "I will get you home, Miss Parris. I will get you home."

• • •

Half an hour later, Lilly was lying on her bed, softly moaning from pain.

Grandmother Rose and Susan stood over Lilly's bed protectively and Susan whispered to Grandmother Rose, "I never seen nuthin' like it. All of a sudden she-"

Lilly covered her ears and began to scream.

Grandmother Rose slapped Susan across the face. "Raise your voice, Susan!"

"I'm sorry. I - I didn't mean nuthin'." Susan started to cry and ran from the bedroom.

Grandmother Rose sat down on the bed, removed Lilly's bonnet and stroked her hair. "You will be fine soon enough, Lilly. This will pass."

"You should not have hit her, Grandmother Rose. She is my friend."

"I behaved badly. Seeing you sick has taken its toll."

Lilly wanted to answer Grandmother Rose but she was suddenly so tired. She shut her eyes and slept until midnight.

• • •

At midnight, Lilly woke with a start and discovered Kyle Edwards sitting on the edge of her bed, watching her. "Kyle, what are you doing here?"

"I went to church looking for you. Then I heard you had fallen ill. I was worried for you, Lilly."

"I am fine, Kyle. Please leave me."

Kyle stood up and walked to the bedroom door. Then he turned and walked back to Lilly's bedside. "Why are you so hard? You give me not the slightest chance."

"You need nothing from me."

Kyle bent down and kissed Lilly on the lips. "I do need you, Lilly. Like I have never needed any other girl. I cannot explain it."

"I want you out of this house, Kyle."

"Please, Lilly. Just give me a chance."

"Go now before I have to call for my grandmother. You will not enjoy her temper when she has been woken in the middle of the night."

"Fine. I will do as you ask and leave you now but I will see you tomorrow night at the Town Hall social and make no mistake, you will dance with me, Lilly Parris. Yes, you will." Kyle turned and quickly walked out of Lilly's bedroom.

Alone, finally, Lilly got out of bed and dressed. She then walked, alone in the darkness, to Bay church. A strong, humid, summer wind rattled the drafty wooden church as Lilly knelt in front of the pulpit and prayed. "Father, tell me what to do. I am so confused. Why will you not guide me?"

15.

SALEM'S TOWN HALL had been lit with lanterns and covered with summer flowers for the evening's festivities and the large, squared log building looked wonderful. Men, women and children, all dressed in their best, crowded into Town Hall carrying baked turkeys, roasted chickens, sweet cakes, and large jugs of ale and wine. Four men on a raised wooden platform played crude musical instruments as Salemites laughed and danced and stamped their feet.

Lilly, in a pale pink dress, stood off to the side, talking to Grandmother Rose, as young men and women danced.

"Why not join the others, Lilly? There is no need to spend the evening with an old woman you see every day."

"I am perfectly happy right here, Grandmother Rose."

Kyle, surrounded by half a dozen beautiful girls, looked across the room at Lilly and Lilly's pink dress seemed to shimmer in the lanterns' light.

Kyle crossed the enormous room and took Lilly's hand. "I would be honored to dance with the most alluring girl in this hall, Lilly."

Grandmother Rose smiled. "I think I can spare her, Kyle."

Lilly frowned. "I would really rather talk with my Grandmother."

Grandmother Rose said, "I will not hear of it. You two have a fine time. I can amuse myself."

Grandmother Rose walked away from Lilly and Kyle and disappeared into the thick crowd of Salemites.

Lilly sighed. "I suppose you will pester me until I dance with you."

Kyle smiled. "Constantly and mercilessly."

"Very well."

Kyle and Lilly made their way to the center of Town Hall and began to dance, awkwardly at first, but, as they slowly moved into each other's arms, their dancing became more and more graceful.

Kyle looked at Lilly and suddenly Town Hall, the beautiful girls, the decorations; all of it faded away, eclipsed, suddenly, by Lilly. "Marry me, Lilly."

"You do not know what you are saying, Kyle. You do not even know me."

"I have never been as happy with anyone else. I have never been so sure of anything. Do not reject me."

"You are not thinking clearly, Kyle."

"Come outside with me. Let me try to convince you."

Kyle took Lilly by the hand and led away her from Town Hall.

"Where are you taking me, Kyle?"

"Patience. You will like it."

Kyle led Lilly through a large grassy field and suddenly Lilly realized where they were going. "Why are you taking me to your father's barn, Kyle?"

"As I said, "Patience.""

Lilly and Kyle entered the large, empty wooden barn and then Kyle walked up wooden stairs that led to a hayloft.

Kyle entered the hayloft, pushed bales of hay together to form a crude bed and then lay down on top of the soft, sweet-smelling hay. Kyle looked down at Lilly who was still standing, nervously, at the barn door. "Come and join me, Lilly."

"I am not sure we should be alone in your father's barn."

"Join me."

"My grandmother will be looking for me."

"She is having a wonderful time. And so shall we."

Kyle stood up and took off his clothes. "I am not ashamed, Lilly. You have already seen me naked. That was no fever dream. That was you in my bedroom."

Lilly, shocked, quickly averted her gaze and stared at the ground, but, then, in spite of herself, she slowly raised her head and looked at Kyle. "Such a handsome body."

Kyle smiled. "Come up here and touch it."

Lilly climbed up the stairs to the hayloft and then stood, stiffly, in front of Kyle, unable to move.

Kyle took Lilly's hand and put it on his bare chest. "Take off your clothes, Lilly. Let me see what you look like."

Lilly hesitated and then took off her bonnet, freeing her long, thick hair. Then, slowly, nervously, she removed her pink dress.

Kyle stared at Lilly admiringly. "Lovely."

Kyle kissed Lilly and touched her bare breasts.

Suddenly, Lilly pulled away.

"What is wrong, Lilly?"

"I have never been - I am a virgin."

Kyle took Lilly's hand. "I will show you how. Lie down."

Trembling, suddenly, Lilly lay down on the bed of hay.

Kyle lay on top of Lilly and began to move. "Do you like it, Lilly?"

"It is not what I expected, Kyle. It hurts. You are so big."

"But do you like it?"

Lilly smiled. "Yes."

• • •

Lilly lay in Kyle's arms and stroked his bare chest. "Kyle, if it is not too much trouble…?"

"Yes?"

"I would like it again."

Kyle laughed and then climbed on top of Lilly. "You healed me and now you will kill me."

16.

THE BRIGHT MORNING SUN illuminated Grandmother Rose's large dining room as Widow Wheeler, Mrs. Black and Grandmother Rose sat in the pretty room drinking tea and stitching a delicate, white, lace wedding gown.

Lilly stood at the window, staring at the herb garden, her arm around Susan. "It is happening too quickly."

"Nonsense, Lilly," said Grandmother Rose. "You will be the most beautiful bride Salem has ever seen."

"Mrs. Black smiled. "You will, Lilly. Your grandmother is right."

Widow Wheeler took a sip of tea. "And for your engagement party, Lilly, I am going to bake my famous ten-layer rum, cocoa cake. It takes almost all day to make but it is delicious!"

Grandmother Rose put down her needle and thread and took Lilly by the hand. "Come, Lilly. Come and talk to an old woman in the herb garden."

Lilly and Grandmother Rose walked to the herb garden and then Lilly, nervous, began to wander around the garden and brush insects from the herbs.

Grandmother Rose said, "We will have the engagement party soon. While it is still lovely and warm."

"Grandmother Rose, there is something you have to know. About Kyle."

"What is wrong, child?"

Lilly frowned. "Look at him. Look at me. Honestly. Does it not seem strange to you? He could have any girl."

"He wants you," Grandmother Rose said, reassuringly.

"Oh, Grandmother Rose, you just do not understand."

Grandmother Rose smiled. "I understand more than you know but we will have no more of this kind of talk. You are going to have a wonderful life. Now come inside. Engagement presents have begun to arrive. You should see them."

Grandmother Rose walked back into the dining room and Lilly followed.

As the two women entered the dining room, Susan, holding an envelope, rushed toward them.

Susan was almost breathless. "This came while you was both outside. By a messenger. The man said it is for me. I never had a letter. Never. Please, read it to me!"

Grandmother Rose took the envelope from Susan, opened it and then removed a letter which she read to herself. "Be calm, child. It is good news from your brother Marcus's master, Peter Andrews. He writes from Boston. He heard of your parents' death and bought your brother passage to Salem."

Susan began to cry. "I barely remember his face. It is a prayer answered."

Lilly threw her arms around Susan. "I am so happy for you, Susan."

"As am I," said Grandmother Rose. "Marcus will live with us, of course."

Susan could not believe what she was hearing and she said to Grandmother Rose, "You are too kind to me."

"Kind and sometimes cruel. Forgive an old woman her moods, dear Susan."

Susan said, "You and Miss Parris could not be better to me if you was my own family."

Grandmother Rose smiled, once again took her seat beside Mrs. Black and Widow Wheeler, picked up her needle and thread and continued to patiently and carefully stitch Lilly's wedding gown.

17.

As Doctor Edwards walked through the streets of Salem and the hot morning sun warmed his body, he thought about poor little Nancy Kelley. If only he could do something to save the girl, to rid her of her horrible pox. Perhaps if he bled her it would reduce her four humors, reduce the amount of blood and phlegm and yellow bile and black bile in her body. That might work; that might just return her four humors to their proper balance. Once the poor girl's blood and phlegm and black and yellow bile were back to their proper levels, Nancy Kelley might regain her health.

Doctor Edwards smiled as the Kelley house came into view. Now he had a plan and he was certain it would work. Now he could offer little Nancy's parents some hope.

A few yards from the Kelley house, Doctor Edwards stopped and checked his medical bag. Yes, he had remembered to bring his razor. He would bleed the girl that very morning.

Doctor Kelley did not bother knocking, he walked right in to the Kelley house and went straight to young Nancy Kelley's bedroom.

June and Harrison Kelley were in the bedroom, standing next to their daughter's bed.

Doctor Edwards nodded to June and Harrison and then he knelt down and pressed his ear to Nancy Kelley's heart. The young girl's heartbeat was irregular and weak. It was too late for the razor, it was too late for a bleeding. The child was going to die, of that Doctor Edwards was certain.

Doctor Edwards frowned and then covered the child with a blanket. "The pox is weakening her heart. The beat is too faint. Try to keep her warm. A chill at this point could finish her."

As Doctor Edwards left Nancy Kelley's bedroom, her parents once again began to cry.

18.

THE MID-AFTERNOON SUN was baking Bay Church. Nevertheless, despite the stifling heat, Lilly was kneeling and praying in front of the pulpit as Kyle entered the building.

"Maybe I will join you, Lilly. I will ask for four wonderful children with you."

Lilly sighed, "You are so sure of everything, Kyle."

Kyle knelt down next to Lilly. "I am sure about this marriage. And so I have something for you."

Kyle handed Lily a small wooden box. "Open it, Lilly."

Lilly opened the box and discovered a beautiful diamond ring.

Kyle slipped the ring onto the fourth finger of Lilly's left hand.

"Thank you. It is beautiful, Kyle. But I have nothing for you."

"Oh, Lilly, do you not realize that now that I have you I have everything I need?"

Kyle embraced Lilly and tried to kiss her but she backed away. "Not here, Kyle. Never here."

• • •

That night, in the hayloft, Lilly and Kyle were naked and locked in a passionate embrace when Lilly suddenly pulled away. "Tell me, Kyle."

Kyle was confused. "Why did you stop, Lilly? Tell you what?"

"There is something I am not doing. There is something you want."

"Nothing."

Lilly would not back down. "What is it you are not saying?"

"Nothing of import."

"I can sense it, Kyle. Tell me what it is."

"A desire I have always had. I cannot speak of it. It is too shameful."

"I am to be your wife. We have no secrets."

Kyle thought for a moment and then whispered something into Lilly's ear.

Lilly recoiled, smacked Kyle's face, grabbed her clothes and hurried from the hayloft.

Kyle quickly dressed and hurried after Lilly.

• • •

An hour passed and, as Lilly sat on an empty dock at the port of Salem with her bare feet in the water, Kyle slowly, tentatively, approached her.

"I thought you would be here, Lilly."

"It appears you were correct, Kyle."

"You despise me."

"No."

"We will never speak of it again, Lilly."

"And the marriage, Kyle?"

"Nothing has changed."

"Now is the time to withdraw, Kyle."

Kyle sat down on the dock next to Lilly and kissed her on the cheek. "We will be married."

Lilly smiled. "We will."

19.

EARLY THE NEXT MORNING, Lilly, Grandmother Rose, Susan and Kyle stood on same dock, staring out at Massachusetts Bay, waiting. (Grandmother Rose held a white parasol - to block the hot morning sun.)

A ship, still just a small dot on the horizon, slowly came into view.

Excited, Susan pointed at the small dot. "There is a ship!"

Kyle frowned. "I do not see anything."

Lilly smiled. "It is coming. I see it too, Susan."

Susan began to cry.

Grandmother Rose said comfortingly, "Susan, this is a time for joy."

The teenager looked at Grandmother Rose. "I am frightened I won't know him."

Grandmother Rose said, "Susan, you will know him. Fear not."

The tanned, muscular, dock master and the scrawny, middle-aged harbor master pushed past Lilly, Grandmother Rose, Susan and Kyle. "Please, everyone, give us room. Ship is coming in," said the dock master.

Grandmother Rose sighed, "It is grand watching the ships dock. It is a sight I have always loved."

"Please, now. We will be wanting room," said the harbor master.

The ship was just yards from the dock now - it lowered its sails and glided towards the dock.

The ship was quickly secured by the harbor master and the dock master and then the passengers began to disembark.

A group of shackled African American slaves hurried off the ship and onto the dock as a large, vicious, slave merchant lashed them mercilessly. The slaves' screams were horrific.

Susan, terrified, attempted to hide behind Grandmother Rose.

The sadistic slave merchant smiled as he spotted Susan, as he saw her fear. The slave merchant quickly moved towards Susan, lunged and managed to grab the teenager's arm.

Susan screamed.

The slave merchant laughed. "This beautiful lass would bring a nice price."

Lilly grabbed the slave merchant, breaking his grip on Susan's arm.

Again, the slave merchant laughed. "Brave girl. Foolish girl."

Grandmother Rose placed the tip of her parasol on the slave merchant's throat. "These girls are not to be touched. Do I need to tell you twice?"

The frustrated slave merchant backed away and then violently lashed Marcus Cooper, a young, muscular slave.

Blood oozed through Marcus's worn shirt but he did not cry out.

The slave merchant lashed Marcus repeatedly.

Finally, Marcus collapsed onto the dock.

Susan rushed to the fallen slave and cradled him in her arms. "Marcus," Susan whispered.

Grandmother Rose approached the slave merchant. "That slave has been freed," she said, pointing at Marcus.

The slave merchant raised his lash.

Grandmother Rose grabbed the slave merchant's arm. "Release him."

The slave merchant backed down and unlocked Marcus's shackles. "You want him? Well, take him then, old bitch! He is useless in any event."

The slave merchant, brandishing his lash, hurried the rest of the slaves from the dock, towards the village of Salem.

Susan stroked Marcus's hair. "Marcus. It _is_ you."

Marcus, badly injured, replied, weakly, "Susan."

Susan and Marcus embraced.

As Susan comforted her wounded brother, Kyle suddenly spotted a young woman of staggering beauty who was disembarking the ship.

Marcus followed Kyle's gaze and said, "Catherine Martin. A school teacher from Boston. Every man on the ship was weak from the sight of her."

"She travels alone?" Kyle asked.

Marcus sighed. "The poor girl's parents died when fire swept through Boston. The beauty is an orphan."

Lilly, suddenly insecure, took Kyle's hand.

Kyle could not take his eyes off Catherine. "All alone in the world. Imaginc."

20.

THE SALEM SUMMER NIGHT was heavy with humidity and the heat in Susan's cottage was almost overwhelming. But the small cottage was clean and well-lit by kerosene lanterns and a weak, (but welcome), breeze traipsed through the small cottage's open windows.

Marcus, still in his worn, blood-stained shirt, stirred a large pot of soup which cooked over a small fireplace. "I brought you a gift from Boston, Susan."

Susan smiled. "I cannot believe you seen Boston. What is it like?"

"It is a wonderful place. One day I will take you there."

"Swear?"

"Absolutely. Now, your gift."

Marcus lifted his worn shirt and slipped a wide, battered leather belt from around his waist. "There is a secret pocket in this belt, Susan. My master made it for me."

Marcus reached into the belt's pocket and removed a tiny bible. "Your own bible, Susan. I will keep it safe and hidden for you. And I will teach you to read it."

Susan was shocked. "You read?"

"My master taught me. In secret. I love to read."

"He sounds a wonderful man."

Marcus smiled. "I cried when we parted. He is a man of great thoughts, dreams and ideas. The men of Boston hate him for his predictions about the slaves."

Susan dipped a rag in water and attempted to clean Marcus's exposed wounds.

Marcus shuddered and moved away.

Susan asked, "What is predictions?"

"His thoughts about the future, Susan. He says one day we will not be slaves. He says our great-grandchildren will have the same lives as white children. He says we will all be equal."

"Marcus, that is crazy talk."

"No, he is a wise man. A dreamer. Susan, I believe him."

The hot, quiet, Salem night was suddenly shattered by the sound of an explosion.

Susan was terrified. "Marcus! What was that?"

Susan and Marcus ran from Susan's cottage just as Lilly and Grandmother Rose ran from the main house.

"Look!" shouted Lilly. "It came from the port."

A cloud of dense, white smoke was visible in the distance, rising from the port of Salem.

Lilly, Grandmother Rose, Susan and Marcus hurried down to the port which was filled with Salemites rushing, screaming, carrying buckets of water.

A makeshift fire brigade had been formed. Men, women and children passed buckets of water down towards a ship that had gone up in flames.

Marcus shouted and pointed at the fiery wreckage. "That was the ship! The ship that brought me here!"

Grandmother Rose stopped an old man as he hobbled by. "What happened here?"

The old man shuddered and then crossed himself. "Struck by lightning. Slave merchant narrowly escaped with his life."

Calmly, Grandmother Rose said, "Lucky fellow."

Marcus was confused. "Lightning? There is no rain or thunder."

The old man nodded in agreement. "Queer business. People are saying it is witchcraft. Take care tonight."

Grandmother Rose said, "Yes, we will lock our doors. We have a wedding to plan. We have no desire to fall prey to witchcraft."

"Grandmother Rose, I do not think witch talk is true," said Marcus.

"I am sure you are right, Marcus" replied Grandmother Rose.

Lilly said, "There are no witches. It is nonsense."

The old man waved his hands, anxious to make a point. "Do not listen to these young folk, Grandmother Rose. Mark my words: witches are real. You lock your doors tonight."

21.

CATHERINE MARTIN WAS IN her kitchen making candles, dipping braided cotton wicking into melted tallow, when Kyle Edwards knocked on her door the next morning.

Catherine yelled, "The door is open. Please come in! I am just now occupied."

Kyle opened the front door, walked through the small house and then entered the kitchen.

"I am Kyle Edwards, Miss Martin. The doctor's son. Well, we heard you were all alone and as yet without slaves so I just wanted to check on you."

Catherine smiled politely. "That is very kind, Mister Edwards, but I assure you, I am fine. My parents are long dead. I am used to making my own way."

Kyle said, "I am sure you are more than capable. I did not mean to offend."

"No offense taken."

"You know, it is rather hot for candle-making today. Why not come riding with me? You will get a lovely view of Salem."

Catherine answered quickly "Oh, how could I? We really do not know each other. I cannot just ride off with young men."

Kyle smiled. "We have just had a very polite conversation. How can you refuse me? I promise you I am a virtuous fellow."

Catherine thought for a moment and then said, "Well, it is rather hot. A ride in the fresh air would be lovely."

"Wonderful!"

• • •

Kyle and Catherine sat on soft, green grass next to a clear brook, eating cheese and drinking wine.

Catherine slowly sipped her wine. "What a beautiful day. I am so glad you rescued me, Mister Edwards."

"I could not let a beautiful woman waste away over a pot of melted tallow," said Kyle as he poured more wine into Catherine's cup.

Catherine blushed. "Such flattery."

"It is not," Kyle insisted. "It is the truth."

And it was the truth. Kyle simply could not believe Catherine's beauty - it was shocking, almost other-worldly. Every time he looked at her, his heart raced. He had never seen anyone so lovely. She was, simply, perfect. And endlessly exciting. And now he had her. She was his. And he would never let her go.

But what if Catherine had not got off that ship? What if she had not traveled to Salem? What if she had stayed in Boston and he had never met her? That would have been a cruel twist. But she had appeared and Kyle knew that he was, without a doubt, the most fortunate young man in the world.

"Perhaps we should go back now, Mister Edwards. I really do have to finish those candles."

"Oh, Miss Martin. Just a while longer, please."

"Well…one half hour. But then I must return to my chores."

"Fine," Kyle agreed. "But you will not work alone. I insist on helping."

Catherine drained her cup of wine. "Your persistence is strangely appealing, Mister Edwards."

Kyle smiled. "I am so glad, Miss Martin. I want to appeal to you."

Kyle poured more wine into Catherine's cup.

22.

KYLE RESTED HIS HEAD on Lilly's bare breast. The air in the hayloft was strangely cool and the summer night was silent save for the sound of energetic crickets. It had been a long, day, it was almost midnight and he was tired. Kyle yawned and said, "I must go home now, Lilly. I need my sleep.

Lilly sat up and looked at Kyle. There was something in his eyes. Something she had not seen before. A coolness. A distance. Quickly, she made a decision. "You are so good to me Kyle and that is why I have decided to give you what you want."

Kyle could not believe his good fortune. "Lilly, are you serious?"

"Get dressed, Kyle and come with me now."

• • •

Lilly took Kyle's hand and together they walked in darkness until they reached Susan's cottage.

Kyle asked, "What about Marcus?"

Lilly responded, calmly, "Marcus walks in the forest every night for hours. He will not disturb us."

Quietly, Lilly and Kyle entered Susan's small cottage.

Susan, naked, covered only by a thin cotton sheet, slept on a straw mattress.

Kyle whispered to Lilly, "I love you for doing this."

"It is what you want, Kyle?"

Kyle smiled. "Yes."

"Then tell me what you wish to see."

"Take off your clothes, Lilly and lie with Susan."

"You will observe?"

Kyle nodded and grinned.

Lilly took off her clothes and slipped under the sheet next to Susan.

Susan stirred in her sleep.

Lightly, Lilly touched Susan's shoulder.

Susan woke with a start. "Miss Parris."

Lilly kissed Susan on the mouth.

Susan moved away.

Again, Lilly kissed Susan on the mouth. "Trust me, Susan. You know I have always loved you."

Slowly, Susan moved toward Lilly.

Kyle smiled.

Lilly and Susan began to make love.

Lilly looked at Kyle and said, "I like this too, Kyle."

Kyle took off his clothes.

23.

KYLE, SHIRTLESS, DRENCHED IN SWEAT, stood in front of Catherine Martin's house and chopped firewood in the hot, afternoon sun.

Catherine walked out of the house carrying two glasses of lemonade. "It is time for a rest, Mister Edwards. You have done more than enough."

"I am happy to continue, Miss Martin, but I will join you for a drink."

Kyle accepted a glass, sat on the ground and loudly gulped the lemonade.

Catherine stood and politely sipped her drink. "I do not know what I would have done without you these past days, Mister Edwards. You have truly been a wonder."

"It hurts me that you will not yet call me Kyle."

"Of course. And you must now call me Catherine."

"I would like that. And one more thing; if you think I have earned it."

Kyle stood and moved closer to Catherine.

"Of course, Kyle. Anything."

Kyle grinned. "Anything, Catherine?"

"Anything within reason."

"I would like to kiss you, Catherine. Is that a reasonable request?"

Catherine turned and walked toward her house. "Perhaps you should go now, Mister Edwards."

"Kyle."

"Go home, Mister Edwards."

Kyle followed Catherine as she walked into the house and made her way to the kitchen. "I could make you happy, Catherine."

Catherine picked up a rolling pin and began to roll pastry dough. "Thank you, I am quite happy, Mister Edwards."

"No, Catherine. You are alone. You are lonely."

"That is not your concern. Now, I would like to roll out two dozen sheets of pastry dough. You really must excuse me. Good day, Sir."

Kyle grabbed the rolling pin from Catherine and then kissed her, forcefully, on the mouth.

Shocked, Catherine backed away and slapped Kyle's face.

Kyle grabbed Catherine and kissed her again.

"Stop," Catherine said.

"I cannot."

Kyle took Catherine's hand and led her to the bedroom where he almost ripped the clothes from her body. "Catherine, you are so beautiful. You amaze me."

"Kyle, please, go slowly," Catherine pleaded.

"I cannot. I want you now."

Quickly, Kyle undressed.

• • •

After two hours of passion, Catherine finally collapsed into Kyle's arms. "I am glad you convinced me," she said with a smile.

Kyle smiled and stroked Catherine's hair. "Let me convince you every night."

"What are you saying, Kyle?"

Kyle, suddenly serious, looked Catherine in the eye. "Marry me, Catherine."

Catherine kissed Kyle.

24.

GRANDMOTHER ROSE'S HERB GARDEN had been specially prepared for Lilly's engagement party. Small tables adorned with linen, crystal and silver were scattered throughout the large garden. In the center of the garden sat a small, raised platform that had been decorated with white and pink roses. The golden, afternoon light of the summer sun made the carefully decorated garden look almost magical.

Grandmother Rose sat at one of the tables stitching a lace tablecloth while Lilly paced, nervously.

Grandmother Rose said, "You are going to pace yourself into a pit, Lilly. You are making me anxious."

Lilly said, "I cannot help it. Everything you have done looks so beautiful. What if it rains?"

"It will not rain," replied Grandmother Rose. "What is really bothering you?"

"I am going to miss you, Grandmother Rose. I am not ready to leave."

Grandmother Rose laughed. "If that is your only problem, I will build you your own house on the property."

Lilly hugged Grandmother Rose. "I know Kyle will love it here. Now we will never be separated."

Grandmother Rose smiled. "You can count on that."

Lilly said, "I love you, Grandmother Rose."

"Sweet Lilly. I love you, too. Now go inside and get into your party dress so I can make a few last-minute adjustments. I want that dress to be perfect and we are running out of time. Guests will start arriving in a few hours."

Lilly ran into the house and then kept running - up the stairs and into her bedroom where Susan was waiting to help her into her white party dress.

With very little effort, Lilly slipped into the lovely dress.

"You are lookin' real beautiful, Miss Parris."

"Susan, I want you for my maid of honor."

"That is not allowed."

"It is my wedding."

"We would be the talk of Salem. No good would come of it, Miss Parris."

"You are my best friend, Susan. Let the good people of Salem say what they will."

"Miss Parris, 'bout what happened 'tween us. Was it something really there or just for the pleasure of Mister Edwards?"

"It was not for him, Susan. At first, I thought it was, but now I know the truth.

"And will we ever…?"

"I do not know. We will have to see."

25.

INSTEAD OF PREPARING FOR the arrival of her guests, Lilly left the house and walked, alone, into the dense Salem forest just as the sun's few remaining rays melted away and darkness rose up to take its place.

As Lilly walked alone in the darkness, lost in thought, she suddenly sensed something moving in the trees. Twigs were breaking, branches were moving. Something was running. Away from her.

Lilly shouted, "I see you, Marcus Cooper. Stop trying to hide from me. Come here!"

Slowly, Marcus left the cover of the trees and moved toward Lilly.

"Why do you run from me, Marcus?"

Marcus said nothing, avoiding Lilly's gaze.

"Look at me, Marcus."

Reluctantly, Marcus looked into Lilly's eyes.

Lilly's eyes narrowed and she studied Marcus's face. "You know something, Marcus."

"It is nothing, Miss Parris. Please. Let me go."

Lilly put a hand on Marcus's shoulder. "Relax now, Marcus."

Marcus, caught, breathed deeply.

"I'm a fool," Lilly said.

"Please, Miss Parris, I want to go - your Grandmother needs my help at the party."

Lilly removed her hand from Marcus's shoulder and he quickly ran off into the dark forest.

26.

ENGAGEMENT PARTY GUESTS CROWDED Grandmother Rose's beautifully decorated herb garden. Susan and Marcus served food and drinks as Salemites talked and laughed under the clear, moon-lit sky.

A small band played softly on the small, raised, decorated platform and party guests danced to the music, twirling in the white moonlight.

Grandmother Rose, resplendent in a blue chiffon gown, kissed Lilly who was clad in the beautiful, simple, white party dress.

Grandmother Rose frowned. "The night of your engagement party and you look nothing but miserable, Lilly."

"Everything is fine. Thank you for all of this, Grandmother Rose."

Grandmother Rose was unconvinced. "And Kyle. I have not seen him all night. His parents, the guests, we are all concerned. You must tell me, Lilly, has there been an argument?"

"There has been no argument. Kyle is occupied at the moment. Shall I get him?"

"Lilly, of course. Get him. This is his party too."

Lilly left her party and walked through fields until she reached Doctor Edwards' barn.

Kyle and Catherine were making love in the hayloft as Lilly walked into the barn.

Catherine, startled said, "I hear something, Kyle."

Lilly raised her voice in the direction of the hayloft. "Miss Martin, I suggest you and Mister Edwards get dressed because I am about to join you."

Lilly would not let Kyle get away with it. She would make him pay. He had completely humiliated her and she would make him pay. He was not going to just cast her aside. If he thought he could get away with it, he would quickly discover that he was terribly mistaken. He had made her a promise and he was going to have to keep it.

Catherine looked at Kyle, confusion in her eyes. "My God, Kyle. Who in the world is that?"

Lilly climbed up into the hayloft.

Kyle and Catherine hurried into their clothes.

Lilly spoke slowly, calmly. "I am going to tell all of Salem how you lied to me, Kyle. How you showered me with pretty words and promises and then used my body. I am going to tell them everything you have done. Everyone will know."

Kyle continued to dress and said nothing.

Catherine could not hold her tongue. "Kyle! Explain yourself."

Still, Kyle said nothing.

But Lilly continued, slowly, calmly. "Miss Martin, does Kyle bring you here often? I honestly thought this hayloft was reserved just for me. I suppose I was terribly naïve."

Catherine looked at Kyle accusingly. "Kyle, have you had relations with this girl? What in heaven is this? Who is she, Kyle? Explain yourself immediately. I will not ask again. Tell me everything now or you will never see me again."

Finally, Kyle spoke. "Oh, Catherine, she is just a sad, lonely, confused girl who has been in love with me all her life. The girl is deluded. She thinks she knows me. Now please, stay here, Catherine and I will end this."

"No, Kyle, I am coming with you," Catherine said.

Kyle shouted, "I said stay here!"

In silence, Kyle and Lilly walked to the party and when Kyle entered the herb garden he immediately strode onto the raised platform and quieted the band. "I would like to say something to all of you."

Suddenly, the party was silent. Everything stopped and everyone stared at Kyle.

Kyle said, calmly, "This marriage will not take place."

The guests looked at each other.

Grandmother Rose put her arm around Lilly.

Susan moved closer to Marcus.

Doctor Edwards took his wife's hand.

Widow Wheeler and Mrs. Black put down their drinks.

Judge Stong said, "Is this some sort of terrible joke, Kyle?"

Kyle's voice was clear and strong. "No judge. I cannot marry a woman of this sort."

Judge Stong was confused. "What do you mean by this, Kyle? What sort of woman do you speak of?"

Kyle said, "I speak of a woman afflicted by the devil. A woman, judge, who practices the black arts. A woman who is, truth be known, a witch!"

The assembled guests gasped.

Grandmother Rose shut her eyes.

Lilly said, "No." It was not possible. It was monstrous. Impossible.

Judge Stong asked, "What proof do you have of these claims, Kyle?"

Kyle took his time before answering. He knew all eyes were on him. He must not seem too eager or too angry. He had to calmly and rationally lay out his case. State the facts and not deal in emotion. Without smiling or frowning or grimacing or raising his voice. He was walking a very perilous path and he had to do so carefully. "I have the most sickening proof of all. You have all heard tales of witches' orgies. Well, the stories are true. I have seen it with my own eyes. And I swear to you it was a sight that made me realize I could never take this woman as my wife."

Kyle paused. He knew it was best not to say too much; he knew it was time to stop talking and let the judge ask him a question.

Judge Stong said, "Be clear, boy. What did you see?"

Kyle paused for effect. It was important everyone thought that it was hard for him to continue. "What I saw Judge, was the surest sign of witchcraft. I caught Lilly Parris lying with another woman: her Negro slave."

The party guests gasped.

Susan dropped a tray of food and attempted to run from the herb garden.

Kyle quickly shouted, "You see, she runs from the truth. She must be stopped!"

Three large men grabbed Susan.

Lilly tried to rush to Susan's aid but two men quickly grabbed her.

Kyle knew it was time to raise the temperature of the crowd. "There! See how the witch attempts to assist her partner in sorcery? They must be driven from Salem before our town is irreparably polluted."

Grandmother Rose threw a large, crystal goblet at the ground, smashing it loudly.

"These are lies, my friends. The boy is an evil, vicious liar."

Lilly pleaded, "Listen to my grandmother, please. Kyle lies. He lies to you as he did to me. He made promises. He took advantage of me. Please. I was a fool to believe him. Do not make the same mistake."

Mary Edwards knew she had to speak up; knew she had to defend her son. Mary Edwards moved close to her husband and then grasped Doctor Edwards' hand and said, "My son is a good boy. He has never lied to me."

Doctor Edwards squeezed his wife's hand reassuringly. He would stand with his wife and son. "My wife is correct. There may well be truth to the boy's statements. Perhaps these young girls do practice the black arts. That would explain, finally, why God has afflicted our children with pox."

Marcus could not believe what he was witnessing. Were the people of Salem mad? It was all complete lunacy. Witches! How could anyone believe such a thing? He could not hold his tongue. "My sister is not a witch. Miss Parris is innocent."

"Silence!" shouted Judge Stong. "We do not take the word of girls and slaves. A young man has made a serious accusation. The matter must be investigated."

Reverend Simpson, a bearded, bespectacled man in his mid-thirties who wore a clerical collar, mounted the raised platform and stood next to Kyle.

Reverend Simpson cleared his throat and then held up one hand, (for several seconds), before he said, "I am deeply troubled this evening, my friends. I came here tonight to celebrate a loving union and, now, we are caught in a situation that can produce nothing but sadness.

"However, the charge is a serious one. If there is even the smallest chance that the devil has infiltrated our precious town of Salem; if there is any possibility that our citizens are practicing the black art of witchcraft, then, we must send word to Boston. We must call for magistrates. We must have a preliminary inquiry in order to determine whether or not there is need for a trial.

"It saddens me to say this but it must be."

Judge Stong nodded his head in agreement. "Reverend Simpson speaks the truth, Salemites. For the good of our village, we must act. We must send word to Boston.

And, until the inquiry, we must detain those accused. If they are infected by the devil, if they practice witchcraft, their magic must be kept at bay."

Doctor Edwards said, "That is only reasonable in this uncertain situation. For the good of our children, these girls must be quarantined."

Grandmother Rose was outraged. "You would put two innocent girls in gaol? On nothing but the word of a liar?"

Judge Stong nodded. "It pains me but it must be."

Grandmother Rose calmly said, "Judge Stong, I do not doubt your sincerity; your wisdom. But honestly, what danger to Salem are two girls? Let us all clear our heads. Let us avoid actions we will, in years to come, regret."

Her family was all she cared about so Mary Edwards knew she had to defend Kyle. "Your granddaughter has obviously attempted to bewitch my son. If she is allowed to roam free she will no doubt try to trick another boy into marriage. The judge is right - she should be locked safely away."

Doctor Edwards said, "Listen to my wife - lock these girls up or our troubles will continue and worsen. Do you people not see? These girls and their evil ways, their magic, their worship of the devil has brought down on our heads a punishment from God. These evil girls are the reason my medicine has failed. These witches are the reason our children are dying."

The crowd murmured its assent.

"Listen to my husband, please," begged Mary Edwards. "These girls are a menace to us all."

Grandmother Rose said, "You are quick to judge, Mary Edwards. You have always been this way. But those who judge are, one day, judged with equal harshness."

Reverend Simpson raised his hand. "This is not a matter for us to judge. This is for church-trained magistrates; members of the general court of the colony. Wise men of Boston."

"The men of Boston have no more wisdom than any of us," said Grandmother Rose. "Please, I beg you all, release these girls into my custody. I will watch them closely."

"No," said Reverend Simpson. "The law is clear, Grandmother Rose. The gaoler must be called when witchcraft is suspected. It must and will be done. Take these girls to Bay church while the arrest warrant is being readied."

A group of men led Lilly and Susan from the herb garden.

27.

THE WARM, LOVELY, MOONLIT NIGHT that once seemed festive had suddenly turned ominous. Bay church was surrounded by armed men with muskets. Inside, Lilly and Susan were seated in a box pew, facing the pulpit. Lilly held her crucifix tightly and silently prayed.

Susan said to Lilly, "Maybe we can climb out a window. I am a fast runner."

"It is no use, Susan. There are too many of them. They have all got muskets and they are watching us. All we can do is wait."

Susan began to cry.

Lilly cradled Susan's head in her arms. "Can you ever forgive me, Susan? I have destroyed your life."

"I do not blame you, Miss Parris. All you done was love me."

"I do love you, Susan. I always will. No matter what they do to us."

"Miss Parris, they cannot do nothin'. It is not true. Witches. Everyone knows it is lies. What could we do to folks? We are just two girls. They will not hurt us. No one will let 'em."

Lilly hugged Susan tightly.

The guards and the gaoler, (who sported a white Elizabethan ruff), entered the church.

The gaoler read the arrest warrant. "Lilly Parris, Susan Cooper, you are accused of communing with the devil for the purposes of practicing his black art of witchcraft. What plea do you enter?"

Lilly took Susan's hand and together they stood.

Loudly, clearly, Lilly said, "I am innocent and my friend, Susan Cooper is innocent."

The gaoler said, "The slave must speak for herself. How do you plead, girl?"

Susan said, "I have not done no witchcraft. I am plain innocent."

The gaoler responded, "The plea is duly noted. Lilly Parris and Susan Cooper will, from now, until such time as this matter is resolved, be detained in gaol as is required by the laws of the general court of this Massachusetts Bay Colony of Salem."

The guards took Lilly and Susan by the arm and led them from the church, through the town of Salem, towards the gaol.

Despite the lateness of the hour, the streets were filled with Salemites: men, women and children.

A young woman holding a baby shielded the infant's eyes as Lilly and Susan passed. The young woman said to the baby, "Do not look, child; you will catch the pox."

The young woman then yelled at Lilly and Susan, "Be gone, witches! Afflict not my child."

A small boy threw a ripe, juicy peach which splattered across the front of Lilly's white party dress.

Lilly pleaded with the crowd, "Please, let us be."

As Lilly continued to walk towards the gaol, she saw Kyle and Catherine standing on the side of the road, watching. Lilly yelled, "Are you proud, Kyle Edwards? Is this what you do to women?"

Kyle whispered something to Catherine and Catherine laughed.

Lilly dropped to the ground and began to scream.

The guards and the gaoler grabbed Lilly, picked her up and forced her along the road.

Lilly shuddered as the gaol came into view. The small, drab, stone building upset her every time she saw it and she had always gone out of her way to avoid it. Lilly tried not to look at the stone gargoyles that were carved into the gaol's entranceway. The hideous stone creatures seemed to leer at her as she reluctantly walked into the building.

As the guards and the gaoler hurried Lilly and Susan through the gaol's entrance, Susan's muscles contracted and her body stiffened with fear. "Miss Parris, I can not be in here. I can not do it."

Lilly heard the terror in Susan's voice and tried to calm her. "We are together. We will be fine."

The gaoler and guards forced Lilly and Susan down a dank, stone passageway that led to a small, dark cell.

Lilly and Susan were pushed, roughly, into the cell.

As the gaoler locked the cell's heavy wooden door, Lilly's eyes adjusted to the darkness. Rats scampered across the dirt floor and water dripped from the damp stone ceiling. The cell's only tiny window was barred.

Susan screamed, "There is somethin' movin' on my foot!"

Lilly calmly said, "It is a rat, Susan. You just hold on to me tonight and the rats will not touch you. They will be gone by morning. That is when they sleep."

Quietly, Susan said, "I am so scared."

Lilly quickly replied, "We will get out. Grandmother Rose will not let them hold us. She will get us a lawyer. Now sleep."

Susan, suddenly calmer, shut her eyes and went to sleep.

Then Lilly shut her eyes. And she too fell asleep. But Lilly had dark dreams. Of something approaching. Something terrible.

28.

As THE SUN ROSE tremulously over Salem, Judge Stong handed a letter to a young man on horseback and said, "I hope I have made clear the importance of this letter. It must reach Boston without fail."

The young man nodded. "Fear not, Judge Stong, you have my word it will be delivered."

Judge Stong nodded and said, "Then off with you. Go!"

The young man raised a riding crop, brought it down on the horse and then rode off into the rapidly strengthening morning light.

29.

KYLE, HOLDING A PICNIC BASKET with one hand, and his fiancee's hand with the other, led a reluctant, slow-moving, yawning, blindfolded Catherine into a small, (but beautiful), field carpeted with orange, red and yellow blanket flowers. Monarch butterflies flew, daintily, around the pretty flowers.

Kyle removed the blindfold and Catherine gasped. "Kyle, it is so beautiful!"

"See, Catherine, are you not happy I woke you early and forced you to come here?"

"Oh Kyle, I think it may be the most beautiful place I have ever seen. How did you find it?"

"I came upon it as a child and I have returned here every summer to glory in the carpet flowers and the butterflies. There is something almost magical about this place. I was going to suggest we get married here."

"Oh no, Kyle, my mother always told me I had to be married in a church. Our wedding must take place in a church.

"However, this might be the perfect place to practice for the honeymoon…"

Catherine winked at Kyle and then began to unbutton her dress.

Kyle laughed, kissed Catherine passionately and then said, "Catherine, we are going to have the most wonderful life."

30.

TWO WEEKS LATER, on a wet, sticky summer night, Boston magistrates Smythe, Tate and Thompson, all in black capes, rode through open fields, shallow streams and dense forests, toward the village of Salem.

As he rode, Magistrate Smythe could not stop thinking about the money he would receive from the Salemites. He had promised his wife that they would add several rooms and new furnishings to their small cabin and finally replace the oiled papers covering the windows with actual glass windows. But to fulfill his promises he would need money. A great deal of money. Glass was expensive, labor was expensive, and the new rug his wife wanted was ridiculously priced! Fortunately, there was a fortune to be made from the eradication of witchcraft. And business was booming - in the last year he had overseen five witchcraft trials. If the money kept coming in, he would actually be able to move from a home built of logs to one constructed of bricks. How proud his wife would be! She would be the envy of all who knew her. A fine home, made of bricks. With multiple fireplaces, ample food and several slaves. Imagine…

31.

AFTER RIDING THROUGH DARK FOREST for several hours, Magistrate Smythe suddenly spotted something unusual in the distance. Some sort of man-made structure. He held up his hand in a way that told his brother magistrates to slow down and then he got off his horse and walked toward the object of his interest carefully, quietly.

When Magistrate Smythe was just a few yards from the mysterious structure his heart raced with excitement. It was a large, wooden, Indian Fort that had been well-camouflaged with twigs, branches and leaves. Oh, the Indians were a devious, execrable race that needed to be extirpated! How clever they thought they were with their insidious camouflage. Well, they were not clever enough. They had been found out. Caught like rats. In the middle of the night. While they slept.

The situation was too perfect, too easy, too delicious. If absolute silence had not been required, Magistrate Smythe would have actually laughed out loud at his sudden good fortune.

Magistrate Smythe whispered instructions to Magistrate Thompson and Magistrate Tate while pointing at three Indian guards who had fallen asleep in front of a small campfire.

Magistrate Smythe studied the sleeping men and recognized the Indian tribe immediately - they were Wampanoag. The sight of them, their dark skin, the deerskin breechcloths they wore between their legs, the feathers they put in their hair, the way they painted their faces with red and yellow ocher, all of it made Magistrate Smythe sick. They were a blight on Massachusetts and they needed to be removed. Permanently.

The three magistrates quickly cut the sleeping guards' throats with hunting daggers.

Next, the magistrates found several large, heavy, wooden logs which they forced, (with great effort), into the fort's entrance gate so that the gate could no longer be opened.

Finally, the magistrates placed a number of long tree branches into the small campfire and then used the burning branches to set the wooden fort on fire.

The fire spread quickly and consumed the Indian fort. Magistrate Smythe laughed as he heard the terrible screams of men, women and children as they tried, in vain, to escape their burning home.

A few agile, muscular young Indians managed to scale the high wooden walls and jump to safety but the magistrates used their muskets and shot the Indians dead as soon as they landed on the ground.

Finally, it was over, the screams died away and the wooden fort was no more.

Magistrate Smythe smiled knowing that he had killed a large group of Wampanoag. He had killed their wives and children. He had burned their food and their clothing. He had completely eliminated them from the earth. He had done good work. God's work.

32.

WHEN THE THREE MAGISTRATES finally arrived in Salem, they rode to Edgley House Inn where they were met by the inn's owner, Jonathan Edgley, a tall, portly, middle-aged man who threw open the inn's front door and ushered the magistrates inside.

Jonathan Edgley said, "Welcome, gentlemen, most esteemed guests! I know you must be tired and thirsty after your very long trip from Boston. Judge Stong and Doctor Edwards have nice, hot whiskeys waiting for you in the barroom.

"I will not bore you with a tour of my establishment right now but if you do not mind my boasting I will tell you that the inn also has a restaurant and, as you will soon discover, a number of lovely guest bedrooms."

The magistrates ignored the innkeeper, removed their black riding capes and joined Doctor Edwards, Kyle Edwards, Judge Stong and Tom Marks at a large, oak table in the middle of the barroom.

As the magistrates walked into the room, Judge Stong stood and extended his right hand in greeting.

The magistrates ignored him.

Undeterred, Judge Stong said, "I am Judge Stong, Henry Stong. Welcome to Salem, good magistrates.

I trust your trip from Boston was pleasant. Please enjoy the hot whiskey while I introduce - "

"Payment is ready?" asked Magistrate Smythe.

The Salemites looked at each other. Finally, Doctor Edwards extracted a small bag of gold coins from his pocket and handed it to Magistrate Smythe.

Magistrate Smythe slowly and carefully counted the gold coins and then said, "You are five hundred short. This is not what was promised."

Quickly, Magistrate Smythe stood up and said, "We'll be off."

Magistrates Tate and Thompson stood up.

Magistrate Smythe said, "Farewell, gentlemen."

The magistrates began to walk away.

Quickly, the Salemites stood up and Doctor Edwards called after the magistrates, "Please, it was our mistake, of course! I am Doctor Edwards, this is my son, Kyle Edwards. The boy will run off right now to fetch the additional five hundred."

Magistrate Smythe stopped walking, slowly turned around and then returned to the oak table where he looked Doctor Edwards in the eye and said, "An additional one thousand."

Doctor Edwards whined almost childishly, "But you just said five hundred."

Magistrate Smythe pounded his fist on the oak table. "Do you think the spread of witchcraft is a trifling matter? Do you think it will be easy to stop the pox; the plague that has descended on your children? We are highly-trained magistrates, expert at spotting the work of the devil. Have you any idea how many months and years we have spent learning our craft? And this is how you thank us? Sir, I must tell you, the way we have been treated thus far is an insult."

Again, the Salemites looked at each other.

Magistrate Smythe knew he had a captive audience, knew the men of Salem needed him, knew he would ultimately get the outrageous amount he asked for and so he pounded his fist on the oak table again and continued. "An additional one thousand is nothing considering how far we have come; what we have and will risk.

"We are here for the good of your town, for the sake of the children. Any citizen of Salem who would begrudge us our due is, no doubt, a practitioner of the very witchcraft we seek to eradicate."

Doctor Edwards had begun to sweat and he nervously said, "You are right, of course, good magistrate. An additional one thousand it is. Whatever we can do, whatever you need, it will be done."

Magistrate Smythe almost laughed. It was too easy. The doctor was a weakling. He should have asked the spineless fool for two thousand.

Doctor Edwards used a handkerchief to wipe the sweat from his shining forehead.

"Go now, Kyle. Get the money. The best money we shall ever spend.

"We will prove to everyone in Salem that your word is true, my son. We will prove the Parris girl and her slave are witches."

Kyle nodded at his father, practically bowed to the magistrates and then quickly left the barroom.

33.

As the magistrates waited for Kyle to return with more gold, Peter Andrews, young and handsome, (despite a deep scar which ran the length of his left cheek), rode, quickly, toward Salem.

Peter Andrews had an extremely sharp eye, even at night, and, so, as he reached the outskirts of Salem and he rode through the thick, dark forest, he suddenly stopped as something caught his eagle eye.

Peter Andrews dismounted and held the reins of his horse lightly as Marcus slowly moved from his hiding place behind a tall oak tree.

Peter Andrews walked up to Marcus and embraced him.

Marcus smiled and said, "Master."

34.

ONCE MAGISTRATES SMYTHE, Thompson and Tate had devoured the roasted chicken and hot whiskey Jonathan Edgley had offered, Magistrate Smythe stood up and said to Judge Stong, "Take us now to the gaol. We will conduct the preliminary inquiry. We will see if there is a hint of witchcraft; if a trial is, indeed, necessary."

Judge Stong said, "At this hour, Magistrate Smythe? Those girls will be exhausted if you wake them."

Magistrate Smythe replied, "It must be done in the dead of night; when the powers of a witch burn bright."

Judge Stong asked, "And what of counsel for the accused? Should a lawyer for the girls not be present?"

Magistrate Smythe smirked. "There is no right of counsel when witchcraft is suspected. The lawyer would become infected.

"No, those girls must be kept isolated.

"Now, to the gaol."

35.

THE THREE BOSTON MAGISTRATES marched, loudly, into the Salem gaol, shattering the still of the hot summer night.

Lilly woke suddenly, opened her eyes and then stood up as she heard the men loudly walking along the stone passageway that led to her prison cell.

Lilly looked at Susan who was still asleep. She wanted to wake Susan, to warn her, but before she could rouse her friend, Magistrate Smythe threw open the cell's heavy wooden door and the three magistrates quickly entered Lilly and Susan's cell.

Lilly recoiled at the sight of the three magistrates, moving as close to the cell's window as possible. Who were these men? What did they want? Their faces were blank, hard, cold. Evil.

Lilly shut her eyes and said a quick prayer. She asked God to protect her. To protect Susan. She asked for help at a time when no one was helping her. She asked for justice at a time when the world seemed endlessly unjust. Lilly prayed with all her might and hoped that, finally, someone would hear her and that someone would answer.

The sudden commotion caused Susan to stir in her sleep.

Magistrate Smythe yelled at Susan, "Up with you now, girl!"

Magistrates Tate and Thompson roughly lifted a sleepy and confused Susan to her feet.

Susan said, weakly, "What is happenin', Miss Parris? Who are they?"

Magistrate Tate smiled an evil smile. "We are here to heal you, girl. Now hold your tongue."

Magistrate Thompson opened a small wooden case which contained rows of long, silver pins. "Now, magistrates, we search for the devil's teat."

Magistrate Thompson handed pins to magistrates Tate and Smythe. "Each time you find a teat, brothers, run a pin through it. Now, strip off their clothes."

Magistrate Smythe tore off Susan's dress.

Susan screamed.

Lilly shouted, "No! Do not touch her!"

Magistrates Thompson and Tate grabbed Lilly and tore off her clothes.

The three magistrates then pinned Lilly and Susan to the ground and slowly ran their hands over their naked bodies. Each time the magistrates found a mole or beauty mark, they forced one of the long pins through the blemish.

Magistrate Smythe yelled, "Who torments you? Who?"

Lilly and Susan writhed and screamed.

Despite the terrible screams, the magistrates continued to insert pins.

Magistrate Smythe shouted, "Who afflicts you? It is the devil. Admit it. You do his witchcraft!"

Lilly managed to scratch magistrate Smythe's face, drawing blood.

Magistrate Smythe smiled and punched Lilly in the face, bruising and blackening her left eye. "Evil girl!" he screamed.

A wave of pain coursed through Lilly's brain. It was a type of pain she had never before experienced. She opened her mouth to scream but no sound came out.

She looked up at the ceiling and saw a large, black spider sitting in the middle of its web. Lilly tried to focus on the spider but blackness began to swallow up the damp, stone ceiling and the black spider.

Lilly felt trapped, trapped by the darkness swallowing everything up, trapped by the unimaginable pain.

Lilly was barely conscious now and the cell and the magistrates were a blur. She weakly said, "Susan…"

Magistrate Tate pushed a pin through Susan's arm.

Susan screamed.

Magistrate Tate yelled at Susan, "Who afflicts you, girl? Tell me. Is it the devil? Tell me and it will be over - I promise. Is it the devil?"

Susan, sobbing, nodded her head weakly and said, "Yes."

Magistrate Tate yelled at Susan again, "Who is it? Say it!"

Susan said, "The devil."

Magistrate Tate smiled. "There! You all heard the confession, my brother magistrates. Given of her own free will."

The magistrates removed the pins from Lilly and Susan and then left the cell.

Susan went to Lilly and held her. "Wake up. They hurt you bad, Miss Parris. But it is over now. I told them all they wanted so it is all over. They promised. You can wake up now. Please. Wake up."

36.

As THE MAGISTRATES TORTURED Lilly and Susan, Grandmother Rose handed a piece of walnut cake to Peter Andrews and Marcus poured him a cup of hot tea.

Peter Andrews looked around Grandmother Rose's dining room. "You have a beautiful home, Miss Parris and you are so very kind to feed me."

Grandmother Rose smiled. "Nonsense. It is very late and you have had a long ride from Boston. You need to eat."

"Thank you, Miss Parris."

"Grandmother Rose, please. It is what everyone calls me."

Peter Andrews smiled. "Grandmother Rose. Of course. Thank you."

Grandmother Rose sipped a cup of tea. "It is I who must thank you, Mister Andrews. Coming all this way."

Peter Andrews said, "I had to come. I have seen what these men can do to young girls. They are pure evil. They claim to do the lord's work. They kill women. Women who are guilty of nothing. For money. I have seen them take the dead woman's property. It is a tragedy."

Marcus poured more tea into Peter Andrews' cup and said, "But what can we do? How do we stop them?"

Peter sipped the tea and then said, "I will testify in court. An expert witness for the accused. I have followed these wicked men from town to town. Once I have told my story, the good people of Salem will do the right thing. Salem is not going to be known for the killing of innocent women. These ridiculous stories of witchcraft are going to stop here and now."

37.

THERE WAS NO SUNLIGHT over Salem the next morning - it was blocked by a thick, wet fog that had swept in overnight.

At Edgley House Inn, Magistrate Smythe, Doctor Edwards and Daniel Flynn sat at the large oak table and drank whiskey.

Magistrate Smythe drained his glass and said, "It is clear sailing now that we have got the preliminary inquiry confession." Of course, we will have the trial - just as a formality. It is all as good as done."

Quietly, nervously, Doctor Edwards said, "Actually. Magistrate Smythe, there may be a small complication."

Magistrate Smythe said, condescendingly, "Trust me, Doctor Edwards, the matter is concluded. I have done this many times so I know far more than you. Now, if you will be good enough to pour me another whiskey…"

Doctor Edwards refilled Magistrate Smythe's glass and then said, "Magistrate, have you ever heard of a man named Peter Andrews?"

Magistrate Smythe slammed his freshly-filled whiskey glass onto the oak table. "I abhor that man! He is famous in Boston for fraternizing with slaves. He has even been known to teach them and free them. A most dangerous man."

Doctor Edwards was almost afraid to go on for fear Magistrate Smythe would lash out or hit him, but he quickly said, "Magistrate Smythe, Peter Andrews is here, in Salem. He followed you from Boston. I have it on good authority he is staying with the old bitch Parris. I do not have to tell you how he could damage a trial."

Magistrate Smythe picked up his whiskey glass and then drained it. "Doctor, this Andrews man must be removed. You must find a way. Everything we have done could end up being for naught if that man is allowed to testify."

Daniel Flynn smiled and said, "Charles Mackenzie made me two new guns just before the wolves ate him. Sad to say for his last effort but the sights on those guns are far off. If I were to wander through the woods and aim, well, the wrong way…there is just no telling."

Magistrate Smythe nodded. "No one could possibly blame you for the shoddy work of a dead gunsmith, Mister Flynn. Faulty gun sights are a terrible danger to us all."

38.

THAT EVENING, just as the sticky, wet fog that had enveloped Salem finally began to dissipate, another thick, yellow, sulfurous, ground-level mist rolled from the fetid swamp to nearby Slaves' Cemetery.

Daniel Flynn and Peter Andrews stood in the cemetery next to a small, lovely marker stone which read: Fisher Cooper 1632-1692 & Leonora Cooper 1638-1692 United in Life; United in Death.

Daniel Flynn said, "It was kind of you to agree to meet with me to discuss the trial, Mister Andrews."

Peter Andrews used a handkerchief to wipe a bit of dirt from Fisher and Leonora's marker stone and then he said, "I just want to help, Mister Flynn. I want to stop these men. That is why I am here."

Daniel Flynn said, "We all want to stop them. Trust me, my good man. I am on your side."

Peter placed a single rose on the Cooper grave and then addressed the grave marker. "Fisher, Leonora, you have wonderful children. Be proud."

Daniel Flynn raised his rifle and squinted as he checked the sight. "Mister Andrews, I wanted to meet here so we could speak privately - safely away from any spies. Let us walk over to the swamp while we talk."

Peter nodded and said, "I thought there must be a swamp nearby. Explains this yellow mist that smells like sulphur."

Daniel and Peter moved away from Slaves' Cemetery and toward the swamp.

The slave-loving man from Boston was a fool, thought Daniel Flynn. He suspected nothing and was blithely walking into a perfect trap. It was almost too easy. Daniel Flynn said, "I will get right to the point. Many people are unhappy that you are currently in Salem, Mister Andrews. Some even say you are trying to interfere with the normal course of justice."

Peter drew an expensive ivory pipe from his pocket and lit it. "Well, with respect, Mister Flynn, those people are wrong. You and I both know full well those girls are innocent. Locking them away, torturing them, destroying their lives is not justice."

Daniel and Peter kept walking as they talked, moving closer to the swamp.

Daniel Flynn said, "Now, be careful where you walk. There is a nasty pool of quicksand just past the swamp. Do you see it, Mister Andrews?"

Peter looked at the large pool of quicksand which was almost five yards wide. "Indeed, I do," Mister Flynn."

Daniel Flynn smiled. "Good. Then I would like you to step into it, please, Mister Andrews." Daniel Flynn pointed his rifle at Peter Andrews.

Peter calmly continued to smoke his pipe. "I think you should put the rifle down, Mister Flynn."

Daniel Flynn laughed. "And why on earth would I do that?"

"Because if you do not, Marcus is going to squeeze the trigger on his musket and blow your head off."

Marcus, standing behind Daniel Flynn, pressed the barrel of his musket against the back of Flynn's head.

Daniel Flynn dropped his rifle.

Quickly, Peter Andrews grabbed the rifle and pointed it at Daniel Flynn. "You must think I am a very stupid man, Mister Flynn. Did you really think I would come out here, the middle of nowhere, unprotected?"

Daniel Flynn was defiant. "You will not testify at that trial, Peter Andrews. Those girls will hang!"

"I will testify at that trial, that witch-hunt. No one is going to harm those girls. You will die long before they do."

Daniel Flynn shouted, "When we get back to town I will personally string you up at Gallows Hill with my own two hands!"

Peter Andrews began to laugh. "Oh, you are not going back to town. Step into the quicksand, please, Mister Flynn."

Daniel Flynn's defiance evaporated and he nervously said, "There is a great deal of money to be made from this trial. It will be no trouble to send a generous portion your way, Mister Andrews."

Peter Andrews calmly, quietly, said, "I have all I need. Step into the quicksand."

Daniel Flynn tried to run but Marcus grabbed him and easily tossed him into the quicksand.

As he struggled and the quicksand began to envelop him, Daniel Flynn screamed, "Please! Do not let me die! I will give you anything you want!"

As Peter and Marcus turned and walked away, Peter shouted, "You condone the torture of innocent girls and now you beg for mercy? Feel their pain, Mister Flynn. Feel their pain!"

The quicksand poured into Daniel Flynn's mouth, as he tried, in vain, to scream.

39.

DARK, OMINOUS STORM CLOUDS had settled over Salem so there was no morning light to aid Doctor Edwards as he entered the Kelley's house in order to examine young Nancy Kelley.

Nancy was asleep in her small bed, clutching her doll. Her breathing was weak. And as Doctor Edwards held up a candle he saw that the sleeping child was now completely covered in hideous smallpox lesions.

Doctor Edwards covered Nancy with a thin blanket and then put a consoling arm around June Kelley. "It is up to God now," Doctor Edwards told Nancy's terrified mother. "All we can do is pray."

40.

LILLY AND SUSAN, shackled, rode through the hot, humid, cloud-covered streets of Salem in a horse-drawn wooden cart. The streets were lined with Salemites who threw rocks and shouted obscenities at Lilly and Susan. One small stone hit Lilly in her tender, black and blue left eye.

Finally, after what seemed to Lilly like hours, the horse-drawn cart came to a stop in front of heavily-guarded Bay Church.

Lilly said, "Oh God, not here. Please, not here."

Two guards pulled Lilly and Susan from the cart and forced them into the large church.

Because of the thick, dark clouds hanging over Salem, Bay church had been lit with candles. The flickering candlelight revealed that every box pew in the church was occupied. Salemites who had been unable to get a seat crowded the church's wide aisle. The entire town of Salem had turned out for the trial.

Two rows of six chairs had been set up at the far-right side of the altar. Twelve jurors occupied the chairs. Next to the jurors, holding a quill pen, sat a court reporter.

Guards pushed aside the crowds and dragged still-shackled Lilly and Susan down the aisle of Bay Church to the base of the pulpit.

Magistrates Smythe, Tate and Thompson, clad in long, black robes, stood on the pulpit with their arms crossed. Each magistrate held a bible.

Magistrate Thompson began. "Lilly Parris, Susan Cooper, you stand accused of witchcraft. Based on the slave Susan Cooper's preliminary inquiry admission of congress with the devil, you will be tried today in this town of Salem. How plead you?"

Lilly said, "You are the devil, Sir. I will pray for you."

Magistrate Smythe said, "Good people of Salem, ladies and gentlemen of the jury, see how the witch tries to remove the focus from herself. A cunning, devilish trick."

"Cunning tricks are your specialty," replied Lilly.

Magistrate Smythe opened his bible and addressed the crowd. "Good Salemites, does the bible not say, 'Thou shalt not permit a witch to live.'?"

The crowd murmured and nodded.

Magistrate Thompson said, "I say now, to both accused, you would do well to confess. A confession will, in the long run, be the least painful path."

Lilly prayed, "Oh Lord, help me. Defend me against these evil men."

Magistrate Thompson said, "Tell everyone. You are witches! That is the truth."

"You are a liar!" shouted Lilly.

Peter Andrews stood up. "Please tell these good Salemites the full truth, Magistrate Thompson.

"Tell them how you bully, brutalize and kill young women for profit. Tell them of your actions in Boston and throughout the colony.

"Tell them how you have tortured these girls. Lilly Parris's eye did not blacken itself.

"Tell them how you fabricate stories which are based on not the smallest kernel of truth."

Peter Andrews sat down and the church was, momentarily, quiet until Magistrate Smythe suddenly said, loudly, "Your facts are false, Peter Andrews and all gathered here know it. But if you insist on proof, you shall have it.

"The doctor's son, Kyle Edwards will stand."

Kyle stood up and Magistrate Smythe addressed him. "Kyle Edwards, you brought these charges based on what facts?"

Calmly, Kyle said, "As stated previously, the witches were caught lying together, moaning with pleasure."

An old woman in the crowd screamed, "Hang them! Hang the witches now!"

Magistrate Smythe yelled, "I will have silence!

"Continue, boy. Tell us how the witch stole your mind and body."

Kyle knew that this was the all-important moment. He was no longer standing in an herb garden at a party. This was a trial. Now, more than ever, he had to make his words believable. He sighed and then looked down at the floor, pretending that he could not look at the assembled crowd, that he was too ashamed. Then, after a full minute had passed, he slowly, bravely, raised his eyes, looked at everyone in the church and told his terrible story. "It was awful, Magistrate Smythe. The lonely witch, Lilly Parris, entered through my bedroom window as I lay sleeping, naked.

"Then, in order to satisfy her base desires, a foul-tasting magic paste was administered against my will.

"Once the magic took hold, the witch used me for her pleasure.

"I was used over and over again that awful evening. I was victimized. As we will all be if these demon girls go free."

Kyle sat down. He tried very hard not to smile but, still, there was a faint smile on his face. He just could not help it, he had done a truly remarkable job.

Magistrate Thompson said, "Now to the boy's father, Samuel Edwards. Doctor, is there further proof?"

Doctor Edwards stood up and said, "Sadly, there is, good magistrate. A story which further illuminates the power of the young witch Parris.

"It was a hunting trip some time ago. The young girl warned our party of impending doom. She made the claim several times; still, we saw nothing. Shortly thereafter, we were attacked by wolves.

"The girl has a black power. She gazes into the future. I have observed her power of divination first-hand and I can tell you with certainty that it is a frightening thing to behold."

Magistrate Thompson asked, "Is this all?"

"No," said Doctor Edwards. "There is also the matter of the destruction of a sailing ship.

"Several people witnessed the Parris girl arguing with the ship's slave merchant.

"Later that evening, the ship was struck by lightning and destroyed. Yet, there was not a cloud in the sky.

"How does such a thing happen? It is unnatural. It is not logical. I am a man of medicine. I thrive on logic but I must tell you that ship was not destroyed by anything logical, it was destroyed by the Parris girl's magic. She cursed that ship the same way she has cursed Salem with pox. She is a menace and she must be stopped."

Grandmother Rose, Widow Wheeler and Mrs. Black looked at each other.

Magistrate Thompson said, "Thank you, Doctor."

Doctor Edwards smiled, politely and then sat down.

Magistrate Tate raised his voice. "Finally, we call on the saddler, Tom Marks."

Tom Marks stood up and said, "These witches tried to murder an innocent babe: my grandson.

"Who would do such a thing? These girls are evil. They pollute our good town of Salem."

Tom Marks sat down.

Magistrate Smythe raised his bible over his head. "'Thou shalt not permit a witch to live!'

"Men and women of Salem, the choice you must make is clear. Consult now, while we all look on. The eyes of Salem are on you. Decide the fate of these witches.

"Purge the town of evil. Do what must be done."

The jury members stood, huddled together and began to whisper.

Lilly's head began to throb with excruciating pain and her vision clouded, causing the jury, spectators and magistrates to quickly fade away. The church began to spin and Lilly started to scream. "Stop it! Stop. Please It is all true; just stop the trial. You are right. I am a witch."

The spectators gasped.

Grandmother Rose, Widow Wheeler and Mrs. Black joined hands.

Magistrate Smythe screamed, "A confession! You have all heard it!"

Magistrate Smythe left the pulpit, walked over to Lilly and said, "Tell us, girl. Tell us everything."

Lilly rubbed her throbbing temples, breathed deeply and wiped sweat from her brow. "I have done things. I have used herbs - to heal; to influence a boy's heart.

"I have forced my slave to lie with me.

"But, please, she is not a witch. Release her.

"It is my guilt alone. I am guilty. God forgive me."

Magistrate Smythe returned to the pulpit. "There can be no forgiveness in a matter this grave.

"Nor can there be release. The witch's consort is equally guilty.

"And, now, I say to you, Salemites, the law of this colony states: 'In matters of witchcraft and devil-worship, a magistrate may by-pass jurors and pass sentence directly.' Therefore, in light of the witch's confession, I declare that these two witches be taken, at sunrise, to Gallows Hill where they will be suspended by the neck until dead. Do you agree, brother magistrates?"

Magistrate Thompson nodded and said, "Agreed."

Magistrate Tate nodded and said, "Agreed."

Grandmother Rose stood and said, "No."

Magistrate Smythe almost laughed. What did the old woman think she could do about the verdict? The girl had confessed. Everyone had heard her. Surely the old bitch had to know a fight was pointless. As a magistrate, he could demand silence but for the sake of propriety it was probably wise to let the biddy speak. God, he could not stand her. She was an annoying, interfering old hag. "Why do you interfere, old woman? The situation is clear. The witch has confessed. There is no other course."

Grandmother Rose spoke slowly and clearly. "Salemites, you have known me and my family for many years.

"Our good work and good name in Salem have always been a matter of pride.

"That is why I tell you now that hanging is not enough. A hanging will allow the stain of this matter to linger. The Parris name must be cleared absolutely.

"These girls must be burned."

The crowd erupted; shouting with glee, hungry for blood.

Lilly yelled, "No!"

Just for a moment, Magistrate Smythe actually smiled. The old bitch had turned out to be an unexpected blessing. A burning would be a fine show and would do wonders for his reputation as a powerful exterminator of witches. Word would spread quickly. Perhaps he would actually have several fine brick houses and even a plantation of his own with dozens of slaves. Imagine, he had almost prevented the old woman from speaking! Without knowing it she had actually handed him a gleaming, golden prize with her withered old hands.

Grandmother Rose continued. "Please, my good magistrate, surely you will understand that only a burning will erase this blot from the earth forever. Once the bodies of these witches are totally destroyed, the Parris family will be able to re-establish its position in the community of Salem."

Excited spectators began to chant, "Burn them, burn them."

Magistrate Smythe said, "You make a convincing case. You have successfully persuaded me, old woman. The witches will be taken to Gallows Hill at sunrise where there will be burned alive."

Appeased, the spectators applauded and cheered and stamped their feet.

Marcus quietly said, "No."

Peter Andrews lowered his head.

Susan, stunned, began to sob. "Please. Do not let them."

Lilly said, "My God."

Magistrate Smythe shouted, triumphantly, "Take the witches away!"

The guards grabbed Lilly and Susan and led them away.

Magistrate Smythe watched as Lilly and Susan were led from Bay Church. And, once again, he smiled.

41.

THE STORM THAT HAD THREATENED the town during the day did not materialize and as night descended, hot, thick, humid air stubbornly refused to release its grip on Salem.

Inside the dank gaol, Grandmother Rose approached the guard who stood in front of Lilly and Susan's cell.

The guard raised his musket. "Stop now. I have strict orders from Magistrate Smythe himself. I am instructed to kill all who try to enter the witches' cell."

Grandmother Rose spoke softly. "I am just an elderly woman. You do not need the musket. Surely, I can do you no harm. You are young and strong while I am old and weak."

The guard did not lower his musket. "There are to be no visitors, by order of Magistrate Smythe.

"I take my orders seriously, good woman."

"I beg you, Sir. I ask for only a few moments to see my granddaughter. I shall never see her again. In just a few hours she dies. Please. I ask for only the smallest kindness."

Still, the guard did not lower his musket.

• • •

Susan was asleep and Lilly was standing at the tiny, barred window, staring out at Salem, when Grandmother Rose entered the jail cell.

Lilly looked at Grandmother Rose and tried, as best she could in the cramped space, to move away. "How dare you come here? Leave me alone. You have done enough. You have killed me."

Grandmother Rose smiled benevolently. "I have saved you, if only you knew it. Come and talk with me, Lilly; there is much you need to know."

Lilly began to cry. "I do not understand. I do not."

Grandmother Rose took Lilly's hand. "You have always known, Lilly. You have always known, deep down. You have always felt it; felt that you were different."

Calmly, Lilly said, "Yes."

"And did you really believe that in all the wide world you were the only one, Lilly?"

"I did, Grandmother Rose. I felt so horribly alone."

"You are not alone, Lilly. There are many, many others like you.

"They cloak what they are; hide their true selves, because they fear they will be shunned by ordinary mortals.

"Still, they exist."

Lilly was defiant. "I do not believe you.

"I have prayed daily. Often two, three times a day.

"I have asked God to change me or direct me to those who share my secrets.

"Yet, despite my constant prayers, I have not changed and I have not met others like myself."

Grandmother Rose smiled. "You speak now to one like yourself."

Lilly was stunned. Slowly, she reached out and touched Grandmother Rose's face. "It cannot be true. You? A witch?"

"Lilly, who do you think sent lightning to the slave merchant's ship?

"Why do you think the guard allowed me in to see you?"

Lilly could not believe what she was hearing. "Then you knew of the love potion I gave to Kyle in the healing paste. All the time you knew I cast a love spell on him.

"So, Grandmother Rose, why in the name of heaven did you not speak?

"You saw, daily, how I suffered. You knew I was tortured."

Grandmother Rose said, "I wanted to shield you, sweet Lilly.

"I wanted your life to be happy and simple.

"Now I know my plan to protect you was a grave misstep. I should have told you the truth from the start."

Lilly said, "You did what you thought best."

Lilly and Grandmother Rose embraced.

Lilly said, "Tell me now, how did Kyle guess the truth?

"And why did the love potion lose its power?"

"I promise you Lilly, Kyle knows nothing. He is and always will be a liar. He does not really think you are a witch. The words he spoke to break the engagement just happened to be true."

Grandmother Rose brushed tears from Lilly's cheeks. "As for the love potion, your magic is still weak; no match for Kyle's black heart.

"But enough of that evil boy; we have urgent matters to discuss.

"I told you once we would never be separated."

Lilly said, "When the sun rises and they tie me to the stake that claim will be proven false."

Grandmother Rose said, "No, Lilly, it will not. We will always be together."

Lilly shouted, "Oh, Grandmother Rose, the fire will consume me! That will be the end."

Grandmother Rose calmly said, "The fire will not harm you.

"Oh, there is much you do not know.

"For hours I could tell you of your powers, what they are, what they will be.

"But now the situation is grave and I must be brief.

"A witch knows, by instinct, all the secrets of nature. Which seeds and berries heal, which insects are poisonous, which herbs can cast a spell. Witches can often see into the future, read minds and, as you well know, witches enjoy lying with both sexes."

"You, Grandmother Rose?"

Grandmother Rose smiled. "In my youth.

"But that is not an issue we have time to discuss.

"We must speak now of the burning."

Lilly looked away. "No. I cannot stand the thought of it. It is too horrible."

Grandmother Rose said, "Look at me, Lilly. And listen to me.

"There are things a witch cannot abide: whispering, the breath of a baby; but a witch will only die if the neck is broken or the head is severed. Hanging would have killed you."

Lilly was shocked. "The fire will not?"

Grandmother Rose said, "The fire will destroy your physical body but your immortal soul will not be harmed. You will return to me, Lilly."

Lilly quickly asked, "And what of Susan?"

Grandmother Rose shook her head sadly. "Susan is doomed. There is nothing that can be done."

Grandmother Rose removed a small, flat, metal container from the pocket of her dress. "Tonight, as Susan sleeps, rub the liquid in this container on her body. It will numb her skin. She will not feel pain as she dies."

Lilly said, "Have you nothing for me, Grandmother Rose?"

Grandmother Rose touched Lilly's face affectionately. "The fire cannot harm you, Lilly. You will feel nothing as your flesh melts away."

Lilly said, "Grandmother Rose, I do not understand. You are so wise, so powerful. Can you not stop this? Can you not save us?"

Grandmother Rose put a hand on Lilly's shoulder and said, "I want you to breathe deeply, Lilly."

Lilly did as she was told and took several deep breaths.

Grandmother Rose shut her eyes and, suddenly, she saw vivid images. Images of herself and Lilly, (now just ten years old), walking together, hand-in-hand, through the streets of Paris.

After a few moments, Grandmother Rose opened her eyes and said, "I have seen the future, Lilly. It would be wrong for me to interfere. What will happen at sunrise must happen in order that we may resume our life together. I know you do not understand at this moment but, please, trust me."

Lilly said, "I do trust you, Grandmother Rose. And now, before I leave you in this life, I ask you just one thing. Please, show me your childhood. Show me the past you have kept secret."

Lilly put her hand on Grandmother Rose's shoulder and then shut her eyes and read her grandmother's thoughts.

Lilly trembled as the shocking sounds and images flashed through her brain:

In 1550, on the Isle of Skye, Scotland, eight-year-old Sarah Delaney carried a straw basket filled with fresh-cut roses and sang as she skipped into Delaney Castle.

The child screamed as soldiers massacred guests at her birthday party.

Sarah clutched her basket of roses, escaped and ran into the forest that surrounded the castle.

Exhausted, cold, soaking wet, Sarah made a bed for herself from wet leaves and, trembling, managed to fall asleep.

Sarah woke up and discovered Jack Parris, an old, bent, toothless man, standing over her, holding a flaming torch.

Jack said to young Sarah Delaney, "What have we here? You are half-frozen, child. Where are your parents?"

Sarah said nothing.

Jack reached for Sarah's flower basket.

Sarah pulled away.

Jack said, "Relax, child. I mean you no harm. I am just trying to see if there is something in that basket that will give me a clue to your identity since you cannot seem to speak."

Jack offered Sarah Delaney his hand. "I am Jack Parris. What is your name, child?"

Young Sarah, trembling, clutched her flower basket and remained silent.

As he was about to ask Sarah another question, Jack suddenly turned around, distracted by the sound of an approaching horse.

The soldier who chased Sarah into the secret passageway rode up to Jack Parris and said, "I search for a young girl. Have you seen a child in these woods, old man?"

Jack shook his head.

The soldier drew his sword and said, "If you lie to me, I will kill you where you stand."

Jack Parris reached out, placed his hand on the soldier's sword, guided the point of the sword to his heart and said, "Do it then. Plunge the sword into me now. Kill me if you will. I am old. I do not fear death. Nor do I have a reason to lie."

Disgusted, the soldier said, "Crazy old man. You are of no use to me."

The soldier whipped his horse with a riding crop and galloped away.

Jack cleared leaves away from a small hole in the ground.

Sarah climbed out of the hole.

Again, Jack offered Sarah his hand and he said, "Your life is in danger, child;

whoever you are. Come with me now. You must leave Scotland."

Sarah took Jack's hand.

Lilly kept her hand on Grandmother Rose's shoulder and shuddered as a new image flashed into her mind:

It was a cold, moonless night and Jack Parris and Sarah Delaney were on a schooner.

Jack looked at Sarah affectionately and said, "The men who sail this schooner are my friends, child. You are safe now. My friends will transport us to the new world."

Jack reached for Sarah's flower basket. "Give me the basket now, child. Look, all the roses are dead. There is no longer a reason to hold on to it."

In a flash, Sarah lashed out and cut Jack's face with her nails, drawing blood.

Jack touched the wound and laughed. "You have a fire in you, child. I like that.

"Child. Child. I must call you something. Yes, the way you clutch those dead flowers. I shall call you Rose. A fine name for a beauty with hidden thorns."

Lilly trembled as her hand left Grandmother Rose's shoulder.

Lilly looked at Grandmother Rose and said, "But that child was born in fifteen hundred and forty-two. You cannot be one hundred and fifty years old. That is impossible."

Grandmother Rose said, "Yet, in your heart, you know it is true. You know I am Sarah Delaney, the young girl whose family was massacred."

"Yes," said Lilly.

Grandmother Rose continued, "I came to Salem with Jack Parris. He cared for me until his death. And after he died, I took the name Parris, forever."

"But why did it happen, Grandmother Rose. Why did the soldiers come?"

"Lilly, my parents were powerful witches.

"They were loved by the people of Scotland.

"They cured many diseases and successfully delivered scores of babies.

"We were happy until the church and the nobles realized they could make a great deal of money by placing their own "healer" in every village. These men charged the people for their services and gave a percentage back to the government.

"Of course, they were charlatans who knew nothing of the healing arts. So, the people shunned them. That is why the soldiers came. The true healers, the witches, people like my parents, had to be killed."

Lilly sighed. "It is so unfair."

Grandmother Rose said, "Life is not fair, Lilly. And much of it, as you know, is horrible. Is it fair that we lost both your parents when they were killed by highway men? Do not bother looking for fairness in life, it does not exist."

Lilly nodded.

Grandmother Rose said, "I must go now, Lilly. Be brave. We will be re-united."

Lilly, fighting back tears, pressed her crucifix into Grandmother Rose's hand. "I love you, Grandmother Rose."

"I love you, sweet Lilly. Now, focus on the time when we will meet again."

Grandmother Rose kissed Lilly and then left the jail cell.

42.

WHEN NIGHT HAD ALMOST EVAPORATED, the door suddenly swung open and magistrates Smythe, Tate and Thompson loudly entered the small jail cell.

Lilly and Susan both woke with a start.

The instant she awoke, Lilly took the small metal container from the pocket of her dress and clutched it tightly.

Still not fully awake, Lilly suddenly noticed that Magistrates Smythe and Tate carried torches but Magistrate Thompson held a long wooden case.

Magistrate Smythe smiled and said, "Just an hour 'til dawn. What a lovely day you have ahead of you, witches!"

Defiantly, Lilly said, "You have your victory. Let us be!"

Magistrate Smythe noticed the small metal container Lilly was trying to hide.

Magistrate Smythe grabbed Lilly's wrist and the metal container fell to the stone floor.

Lilly screamed, "No! It is mine. Give it to me!"

Magistrate Smythe picked up the metal container, threw it out the window and then smacked Lilly's face.

"The evil potion it contained will not help you now, girl."

Lilly began to cry. "Susan, forgive me."

Magistrate Smythe punched Susan in the face.

Susan screamed.

Magistrate Thompson opened the wooden case and removed a long, iron handle which had, affixed to its end, a large iron capital letter B. Magistrate Thompson put the iron B into the flame of magistrate Tate's torch.

One minute passed and then the iron B began to glow red.

Susan asked Lilly, "What are they doing?"

Magistrate Smythe took the glowing red poker from Magistrate Thompson and smiled. "You will now be labeled for what you are: demons who have bewitched Salem."

Magistrate Thompson grabbed Lilly's head.

Magistrate Tate grabbed Susan's head.

Magistrate Smythe moved toward Susan.

Susan yelled, "No! Do not do it!"

Magistrate Smythe pressed the red-hot B against Susan's forehead.

Susan screamed and her flesh smoked and then the metal was withdrawn to reveal a perfect B brand.

Magistrate Smythe smiled and moved toward Lilly.

Lilly's eyes narrowed and she calmly said, "I curse you. You will burn in hell, all three."

Magistrate Smythe laughed. "No, my little witch. In just a few minutes, it is you who will burn."

Magistrate Smythe pressed the B against Lilly's forehead.

43.

As the sun rose over Salem, Lilly and Susan, shackled, rode towards Gallows Hill in a horse-drawn, wooden cart.

Excited Salemites lined the route to Gallows Hill.

Susan, crying, said to Lilly, "I never got to see Boston."

Lilly calmly said, "They will pay for this crime, Susan. I promise you that."

As the horse-drawn cart climbed to the top of Gallows Hill, Lilly saw that a large crowd had gathered around two enormous pyres of straw, twigs and kindling wood. A long wooden stake had been stuck through each pyre.

As the cart approached, Magistrate Smythe, standing amongst the crowd, yelled, "Look, Salemites! The witches draw near! Now we shall kill the evil that surrounds us."

The crowd cheered.

Grandmother Rose, Mrs. Black and Widow Wheeler bowed their heads in prayer.

Marcus held Susan's small bible and quietly stood next to Peter Andrews.

Kyle, Catherine, Doctor Edwards and Mary Edwards, pointed at Lilly and Susan and whispered.

The cart carrying Lilly and Susan came to a stop in front of the pyres.

Magistrate Smythe said, "Let us bow our heads in prayer."

Magistrate Smythe paused for dramatic effect before he spoke. He wanted everyone present to remember, precisely, every single thing he did. So, he paused. And as he paused, he knew, with great certainty that every moment and, in fact, the entire day, the entire trial, would be remembered by all, he knew he would be a legend, a legendary witch-killer. He would be praised and applauded and respected and rewarded and feared. He knew, absolutely, that Salem would be forgotten but that he would be remembered. The great eradicator of witchcraft would be remembered!

Finally, when the moment was right, Magistrate Smythe said, "Lord God, through your mercy, may those who have lived in sin now find eternal peace.

"Bless this purification and send your angels to watch over it as we drive the devil from the bodies of Lilly Parris and Susan Cooper.

"Lift your punishment. Lift the pox from the town of Salem. Free the dying children.

"Welcome these witches into your presence and with our saints let them rejoice forever.

Amen."

Guards unshackled Lilly and Susan and dragged them to the pyres; chaining them to the wooden stakes.

Tom Marks screamed, "Burn them!"

The crowd cheered in agreement.

Judge Stong, standing next to Tom Marks, put a hand on Marks' shoulder in an attempt to quiet Tom.

Magistrates Tate and Thompson raised their hands over their heads.

Magistrate Tate yelled, "What we do now is the Lord's work!"

Again, the crowd cheered.

Magistrate Thompson yelled, "Never again will the town of Salem know the evil that is witchcraft!"

Magistrates Tate and Thompson climbed onto the pyres, dipped crude brushes into pails filled with animal fat and then painted Lilly and Susan with the fat.

Marcus pushed through the crowd and handed Susan's small bible to Reverend Simpson.

Marcus whispered something into the reverend's ear.

Reverend Simpson climbed up onto the pyre where Susan was shackled and pushed the small bible into the chains that bound Susan to the wooden stake.

Magistrate Smythe lit a torch and then held it in the air.

The crowd screamed.

Magistrate Smythe smiled and touched the flaming torch to each of the pyres.

The pyres caught fire and the flames and smoke slowly rose upward.

Susan's ragged dress caught fire.

The pain was unbearable. Susan screamed.

Lilly's clothes began to burn.

The crowd cheered.

The flames rose into the air, enveloping Lilly and Susan.

Susan tried to find her brother in the crowd, tried to find Marcus, but her vision was blocked by smoke and flames and everything began to fade away.

As thick white smoke choked her, she writhed in agony and slowly lapsed into unconsciousness.

Susan's flesh hissed and blistered as she was burned alive.

Lilly felt nothing and she could see clearly. The cheering crowd and Susan's charred corpse were clearly visible through the smoke and flames.

"A curse on this town, a curse on Salem," Lilly managed to say before her flesh quickly melted away, exposing white bone.

• • •

Lilly Parris looked down on Salem through wispy white clouds as the village and its citizens became smaller and slowly faded away.

The air was now her domain.

She felt no physical sensations. She felt nothing. No pain, no hunger, no fatigue, no thirst.

But she saw everything.

And she could travel anywhere. She could race across the heavens in a flash. She was completely unburdened. Everything was effortless. She was everywhere. She was nowhere. She was darkness. She was light. Space and time meant nothing to her. One minute. One hour. One day. One week. One inch. One foot. One yard. One mile. It was all as nothing to her. She was completely and totally free. A free spirit.

• • •

The large crowd gathered around the pyres lost interest once the flames died away. There was nothing left to see but ash and bone.

Bored Salemites slowly wandered away from the scene of the executions and then unpacked picnic baskets and began to eat and laugh and talk.

• • •

When the burning sun had set and Gallows Hill was safely cloaked in darkness, Grandmother Rose walked back to the top of the hill, climbed onto Lilly's still smoking pyre, carefully collected Lilly's bones and then placed them into a large wicker basket.

44.

MAGISTRATES SMYTHE, TATE and Thompson were proud of themselves. They were local heroes who had had a very productive day. They had burned two witches and then they had joined several families for a wonderful, all-day picnic of freshly-baked bread, hardboiled eggs, roasted venison, strawberries, apples, quince pies and beer. Their dining companions had spent hours complimenting them on the fine job they had done ridding Salem of witchcraft. And when the picnic finally ended and the burning sun began to set, they had returned to Edgley House Inn to continue the celebration with hot whisky at the large oak table in the center of the barroom.

Magistrate Smythe raised his glass and toasted his companions. "My brother Magistrates, I could not ask for better or more capable confidantes. You have both performed capably, competently, and, I must say, admirably. I could not have chosen two better partners for this endeavor. You are both great friends to me and I say to you both: let us all three drink to a job well done."

The three magistrates quickly drained their glasses of whiskey and then loudly pounded their glasses on the table.

Quickly, a fawning, obsequious Jonathan Edgley refilled the magistrates' glasses. "No charge for this round of whiskey, my dear Magistrates. All of Salem is talking of the marvelous way you burned the evil witches this morning."

The magistrates cheered, quickly drained their glasses and then once again began to loudly pound on the oak table.

• • •

While the three magistrates celebrated, Grandmother Rose stood in her herb garden which was well-lit by flickering tapers and the bright light of the hot summer moon. Using a long, wooden stick, Grandmother Rose scratched a perfect picture of Edgley House Inn into the dirt.

• • •

Comfortably drunk, Magistrate Smythe raised his glass of whiskey and, again, toasted his fellow magistrates. "This is only the beginning, brother magistrates. We will rid this entire country of witchcraft. There is no telling how many witches we will uncover and exterminate on our travels.

"There is no telling how successful we will become. Sooner than you can even imagine, we will be adjudicating a witch trial each and every week.

"There will be no end to the rewards. We will all own the finest clothes, the finest homes. Our wives and children will wear the softest leathers and silks. We will all have multiple properties and slaves."

Magistrate Smythe took two gold coins from his coat pocket and handed one coin to Magistrate Tate and one coin to Magistrate Thompson.

Magistrates Tate and Thompson smiled and patted Magistrate Smythe on the back and told him he was a fine fellow.

And once again, the magistrates cheered and pounded on the oak table and called for more whiskey.

• • •

By the light of the tapers and the moon, Grandmother Rose poured kerosene on the picture she'd drawn of Edgley House Inn and said, "Burn in hell."

• • •

Magistrate Smythe suddenly put down his glass of whiskey and asked his fellow magistrates, "What is that horrible smell?"

• • •

Grandmother Rose touched a burning taper to the kerosene-soaked picture of Edgley House Inn and the kerosene ignited.

• • •

As the magistrates sat at the large oak table, drinking glasses of whiskey, the walls of Edgley House Inn burst into flames.

Magistrates Smythe, Tate and Thompson were, suddenly, engulfed in flames.

Magistrate Smythe screamed, "Help me!"

The three magistrates screamed as their clothes ignited.

Flames shot from the windows of Edgley House Inn.

Jonathan Edgley and the three magistrates pulled and pulled on the Inn's front door, trying, in vain to escape.

No one succeeded - the door would not budge and Jonathan Edgley, Magistrate Smythe, Magistrate Thompson and Magistrate Tate were all quickly consumed by the fire.

45.

MARCUS AND PETER ANDREWS did not hear the screams from Edgley House Inn as they walked through Slaves' Cemetery.

When Marcus came to his parents' headstone, he got down on his hands and knees and brushed dust and dirt from the stone.

Peter Andrews put a hand on Marcus's shoulder. "The memories will haunt you here, Marcus. Come back to Boston. You can live with me a free man."

Marcus had tears in his eyes as he looked up at Peter Andrews. "It is so generous, Peter. You are a good person. I will come with you but not just yet. Let us stay a while in Salem."

"Marcus, why would you want to stay in Salem? After what it has done to your family."

Marcus smiled, sadly, and said, "Just a feeling."

46.

TIME NO LONGER MEANT anything to Lilly Parris so she did not really understand that two weeks had passed since her mortal body had been burned at the stake on a pyre at Gallows Hill in the year sixteen hundred and ninety-two.

But she did, vaguely, remember her home in Salem and a kind, elderly woman and a wonderful, doomed friend and a handsome, treacherous lover.

And though she felt buoyant and joyous and adored her new-found freedom, though she loved sailing, care-free on the wind, though she loved whirling through the rain and the fog and the mist and though she could have traveled anywhere in the world, anywhere in the heavens, something kept pulling her back towards the home she'd abruptly left, some powerful, invisible, mysterious thread kept tugging her back in the direction of Salem. No matter how high or how far away she flew in her wonderful new spirit form, something kept calling her back.

Why she was being called back, Lilly did not know. But she sensed that something was unfinished.

47.

CATHERINE MARTIN HAD ONLY BEEN given two weeks to prepare for her wedding. She and Kyle had set the date on the very day evil Lilly Parris and her foul slave had been burned. Actually, that was not quite true, they had not agreed on the date together. In truth, what had transpired was: as the monstrous Lilly Parris was tied to the stake and set on fire, Kyle had smiled and whispered, "Catherine, I shall marry you at Bay Church in exactly two weeks. Make all the preparations. Cost be damned!"

And now the magical day had finally arrived! Catherine thought of everything she had accomplished in just two weeks.

Without money, it would have been impossible. So, it was fortunate that Kyle's father was rich. Had she fallen in love with a poor man, the wedding gown would not have been so quickly sewn, the magnificent flowers, (hundreds of white roses), would not have been so quickly delivered from Boston, the china, the silver, the crystal, the sweet, delicate, intricate, wedding cake, the mountain of food and drink for the guests, none of it would have materialized if Kyle's father had not parted with a considerable amount of gold.

Kyle confided to her that his father never hesitated to use his fortune to make his son's life better. Doctor Edwards did not mind paying for the lavish wedding Kyle wanted. Nor did the good doctor object to parting with gold when magistrates had to be hired in order to prove to the good people of Salem that Kyle had been tricked and bewitched by black-hearted sorceress Lilly Parris.

Catherine had never been happier and she could not stop smiling as she and Kyle rode toward Bay Church in a beautiful horse-drawn carriage that had been decorated with white roses.

Catherine thought she was going to cry with joy when the horse finally stopped in front of Bay Church and Kyle, dressed in full morning dress, took her hand and helped her from the carriage.

She felt like a princess!

48.

As the horse finally stopped in front of Bay Church, Kyle took Catherine's hand and helped her from the carriage. Look at her, thought Kyle. She truly was magnificent!

How lucky he had been to escape his engagement to Lilly Parris. Imagine being married to a plain woman. The thought of it actually made him feel sick. How lucky he had been to concoct a story that was believed by all of Salem. Actually, luck had little to do with it. He had always been an artful liar. Even as a child he had known exactly what to say in order to make people believe him. It was a skill he had been born with and he had honed it to perfection. Some could sing, some could draw, he could lie. It was a wonderful skill and he had used it to great advantage. He was about to acquire a magnificent bride, the most beautiful girl he had ever seen. They would have beautiful children and their family would be the envy of Salem. It would be a perfect life. He really was the luckiest man in the world.

Kyle smiled at his bride-to-be and said, "My dearest Catherine, you are, truly, a vision. I cannot believe you arc going to be mine forever. Now come inside the church and marry me. I cannot wait another moment."

Kyle kissed Catherine's cheek and led her into a church that was filled with well-wishers and white roses.

49.

THE SUN SHONE BRIGHTLY over Salem as Kyle Edwards and Catherine Martin walked into Bay church. The heavy, wet, oppressive summer air that had suffocated Salem for weeks had finally lifted and a fresh, pleasant breeze wafted through Bay Church, comforting the wedding guests.

As Kyle and Catherine slowly made their way down the center aisle of the church, Mary Edwards, sitting in a box pew, said to her husband, "Oh, Samuel, look how handsome our boy is. And Catherine. Such beauty. And that gown. And the way her hair is upswept and adorned with delicate sprigs of baby's breath. I have never seen such a vision."

Doctor Edwards smiled and squeezed his wife's hand. "She truly is remarkable. Leave it to our clever son to marry such a beauty. Imagine the grandchildren she will produce. When I think of what we almost ended up with I have to breathe a sigh of relief."

"I know, Samuel. It is wonderful how everything worked out. Thank God."

Kyle and Catherine came to a stop when they reached Reverend Simpson, who was smiling and waiting for them in front of the pulpit.

Reverend Simpson opened his bible and then addressed Kyle. "Will you, Kyle Edwards, take this woman, Catherine Martin, to be your wife for as long as you shall live?"

Kyle looked at Reverend Simpson with fondness. Such a kind, avuncular man. Kyle smiled and was about to open his mouth when he noticed something that seemed to be hovering in front of Reverend Simpson's face. It was something that was there yet not quite there. It was gauzy, filmy, ethereal. Yet it had a face. And it was smiling at him. And the face looked like Lill-

No! It was impossible. Kyle's heart began to pound and he started to sweat. His legs felt as though they could no longer support him. He fell forward and grabbed onto Reverend Simpson for support.

Catherine screamed, a horrified Mary Edwards covered her mouth with one hand and the wedding guests gasped.

Reverend Simpson quickly helped Kyle to his feet and then addressed the Salemites. "My dear friends, if I had a piece of gold for every groom I have seen faint on his wedding day, I would be a wealthy man."

The wedding guests roared with laughter.

Kyle quickly wiped his sweaty forehead with a handkerchief.

Reverend Simpson said, "Now Kyle, are you ready to be joined in holy matrimony with the woman for whom you fell?"

Again, the guests laughed.

Kyle looked at Reverend Simpson. The kind old man looked normal now. The disturbing vision was gone.

Kyle breathed, deeply. And then nodded.

Reverend Simpson said, "Will you, Kyle Edwards, take this woman, Catherine Martin, to be your wife for as long as you shall live?"

Kyle said, "I will."

Reverend Simpson continued. "And will you, Catherine Martin, take this man, Kyle Edwards, to be your husband for as long as you shall live?"

Catherine smiled and said, "I will."

Reverend Simpson cleared his throat.

Kyle understood the signal and quickly removed a ring from the pocket of his morning coat. Kyle then handed the ring to the reverend.

Reverend Simpson held up the ring and said, "This ring is a symbol of your love. Of your dedication. I bless it now, in the name of God."

Reverend Simpson handed the ring back to Kyle.

Kyle slipped the ring onto the fourth finger of Catherine's left hand.

Reverend Simpson said, "If no one can now show a reason why these two should not be joined in holy matrimony, I pronounce that they are, under the laws of God and this Bay Colony of Salem, man and wife.

"The couple may kiss."

Kyle and Catherine kissed.

The assembled Salemites cheered.

Mary Edwards kissed her husband. "This is surely the happiest day of my life, Samuel."

Doctor Edwards hugged his wife. "And things will only get better, Mary."

Kyle and Catherine turned away from Reverend Simpson and, then, laughing and holding hands, they rushed back down the aisle of Bay Church as Salemites showered them with rice and rose petals.

As Kyle and Catherine left Bay Church, Kyle shouted, "On to our wedding party, my wife! Today we spend in celebration!"

50.

"CATHERINE EDWARDS. CATHERINE EDWARDS. I will never again be Catherine Martin. I am Catherine Edwards now. Can you believe it?"

Kyle laughed. He kissed Catherine's cheek and said, "What I cannot believe is this wondrous wedding party you arranged. I have never seen Town Hall look so marvelous. It is absolutely enchanting."

It was true - Town Hall's squared log interior had been transformed. It was no longer a large, drab, empty space. It was now filled with red, white and yellow roses and the scent of flickering white, lemon-scented candles. Town Hall had been stocked with what seemed like an endless supply of food and drink, (surely enough to last all day and night), and the well-dressed, energetic young musicians had been instructed to play until the last, tired wedding guests finally staggered off into the moonlight.

Kyle took Catherine's hand and slowly they began to dance. "Let us just dance and drink and laugh and eat today."

"And tonight?" asked Catherine.

Kyle smiled. "Tonight, we will leave this party and have a different kind of fun."

51.

THAT NIGHT, the sounds of the Town Hall wedding celebration could be heard by Marcus, Grandmother Rose, Widow Wheeler and Mrs. Black, who were all gathered in Grandmother Rose's herb garden.

As Marcus added wood to a fire that burned under a large, metal, water-filled kettle, Mrs. Black and Widow Wheeler moved slowly through the garden, gathering herbs in wooden bowls.

Grandmother Rose stirred the boiling cauldron as Mrs. Black and Widow Wheeler tossed in the herbs they had collected.

Grandmother Rose said, "Take your time, ladies. I want this spell to be perfect. I am sure we all do."

Grandmother Rose adjusted a log on the fire. "We will need more wood, Marcus. We want to keep this nice and hot. It has to burn all night."

Marcus hurried off in search of more firewood.

Mrs. Black and Widow Wheeler added more herbs to the pot as Grandmother Rose reached into the pocket of her dress. "How say you, ladies?"

Mrs. Black said, "Do it, Grandmother Rose."

Widow Wheeler nodded and said, "Do it."

Grandmother Rose pulled a single, live leech from the pocket of her dress, tossed it into the cauldron and said, "Judge not, lest ye be judged."

Marcus returned, carrying firewood. Quickly, he added another log to the fire.

Grandmother Rose lifted her hands into the air and began to hum and spin. "I feel vibrant tonight, ladies. I have the energy of a young girl."

Mrs. Black said, "Conserve that energy. It will be a long night."

Grandmother Rose stopped spinning, shut her eyes and breathed deeply. "Now, Marcus, go into my bedroom and bring the wicker basket on my nightstand. And when you are done, there is one last thing I will need."

52.

WHILE THE DAZZLING SUMMER moon shone down on Salem and the wedding guests continued to celebrate, Kyle grabbed Catherine's hand and quickly led her out into the warm night air. The newlyweds ran, laughing, away from Town Hall, and they did not stop running and laughing until they reached Catherine's small house.

Catherine asked, "Are we not going to sleep at your parents' house tonight?"

Kyle said, "No, we will move there eventually, but our honeymoon shall be spent here - this house will afford us total privacy."

Kyle took Catherine's hand, led her into the bedroom and then kissed her on the lips. "You were the most beautiful bride Salem has ever seen."

Catherine ran her hands through Kyle's thick hair. "It was a wonderful wedding but I wanted to be alone with you, Kyle. I am so glad you brought me here; that party will go on all night."

"If my parents had their way, we would still be at that party. Now, take off your wedding dress."

Slowly, Catherine began to undress.

Kyle grabbed Catherine and ripped the dress off her body.

"Kyle! I was hoping to preserve that dress for our daughter."

Kyle hurried out of his clothes. "Let me make a daughter."

Kyle picked Catherine up and threw her onto the bed.

Catherine laughed and screamed.

53.

IT WAS HAPPENING AGAIN. Something was pulling Lilly back. Back to Salem. As she drifted, aimlessly, happily, contentedly, through the warm night air, Lilly could sense a kindly old woman. Had she known the old woman somehow? Lilly thought so but she was not entirely sure. Perhaps the woman had been a relative or a parent. Whatever the connection had been, Lilly sensed that the old woman had cared for her deeply. And continued to care for her. There was a bond between them, of that Lilly was certain. And it was that bond, that string that kept pulling her back. Lilly suddenly knew that, felt that, understood that, with great clarity and certainty. The kind old woman was the one pulling her back to Salem. With her thoughts. Yes, that was it, the old woman was thinking about her. Constantly. That was why she could not completely break away from Salem. That was why she kept returning and hovering over the village where she had once lived in a completely different form - a solid, mortal form. Lilly wanted to break away completely, wanted to fly free, to soar into the heavens and never return but she could not. For reasons Lilly simply did not understand, the old woman would not let her go.

54.

MARCUS CHECKED THE FIRE and, then, when he was satisfied, he handed Grandmother Rose the wicker basket.

Grandmother Rose asked, "Who has the mortar and pestle?"

"I have it," said Mrs. Black.

Mrs. Black handed the mortar and pestle to Grandmother Rose.

Grandmother Rose opened the wicker basket, reached inside and removed a white bone. She placed the bone in the mortar and then used the pestle to grind the bone into powder.

Widow Wheeler said, "Grind it well, Grandmother Rose. It must be pure powder. This is a delicate spell. There must not be even a single chip."

Finally satisfied, Grandmother Rose stopped grinding the bone and then tipped the mortar over the cauldron and carefully sprinkled the powdered bone into the boiling herbs. She then reached into the wicker basket, removed another bone and, again, began to grind with the pestle. "Fear not, Widow Wheeler, this spell is going to be our greatest success."

Widow Wheeler and Mrs. Black smiled and joined hands.

Widow Wheeler said, "Come back to us."

Mrs. Black said, "Come back."

Silently, Marcus tended to the fire.

• • •

Mary Edwards, dressed in her nightclothes, stood next to the bed and brushed her hair. It was hard to even hold the brush - she was completely exhausted. The wedding service and the subsequent all-day, (and almost all-night!), party had absolutely drained her. She yawned and said to her husband, (who was already lying on the bed), "I barely have the strength to get myself into our bed, Samuel. This wonderful day has taken quite a toll."

Doctor Edwards said to his wife, "Come and keep me warm, Mary. You will be refreshed in the morning. I will cook your favorite breakfast."

Mary laughed and kissed the top of her husband's head. "You will cook? That will be a sight to see - one I have never seen before."

Mary extinguished the flame of a kerosene lamp and the bedroom was plunged into darkness.

Doctor Edwards muttered as he fell asleep, "You will see it in the morning, Mary. You will see…"

• • •

Lit by the moon, which shone in through the bedroom window, Kyle and Catherine, naked on the bed, made love on their wedding night.

Kyle, sweating, moaned and rolled off Catherine.

Catherine's forehead was beaded with perspiration. There was a strange look in her eye. "I want you again, Kyle."

Kyle, breathing heavily said, "Give me a moment, Catherine."

"Please, Kyle. It has to be now. I can feel it."

• • •

Grandmother Rose continued to add powdered bone to the boiling cauldron. "Come back to me, Lilly. Come back now."

• • •

Catherine got on top of Kyle and reached between his legs.

Kyle moaned.

"Now, Kyle."

• • •

Marcus put another log on the white-hot fire.

Mrs. Black and Widow Wheeler stirred the cauldron.

Grandmother Rose stretched her arms heavenward. "Come to me now, Lilly."

Grandmother Rose squeezed her eyes shut and began to moan.

• • •

Catherine, still on top of Kyle, shut her eyes and moaned with pleasure.

Kyle, soaked with sweat, squeezed his eyes shut and he, too, began to moan.

Catherine arched her back.

• • •

Grandmother Rose said, "Now, Lilly."

• • •

Kyle arched his back and shuddered.

Catherine squeezed her eyes shut and screamed with pleasure.

• • •

Grandmother Rose screamed and collapsed onto the ground.

Grandmother Rose was short of breath, but as her breathing quickly returned to normal, she saw a glassy, crystalline, ghostly form materialize in the herb garden. The form was barely visible but Grandmother Rose knew that it was Lilly.

Marcus rushed to Grandmother Rose and helped her to her feet while Mrs. Black and Widow Wheeler continued to stir the cauldron.

Grandmother Rose smiled and said, "It is done, witches. Lilly's immortal soul has returned to us. I can see it."

• • •

Kyle and Catherine collapsed into each other's arms.

Catherine said, "There is a child, Kyle. I am sure of it."

Kyle kissed Catherine. "If it is true, let it be a daughter. Let it be as lovely as its mother."

• • •

As Marcus silently observed, Grandmother Rose, Widow Wheeler and Mrs. Black held hands, hummed and slowly circled the cauldron in a counter-clockwise motion.

"Judge not," said Mrs. Black.

"Lest ye be judged," said Widow Wheeler."

• • •

The bedroom was dark and quiet and Doctor Edwards and Mary Edwards slept soundly.

• • •

Grandmother Rose placed her right hand over Widow Wheeler's mouth and her left hand over Mrs. Black's eyes.

• • •

Mary Edwards began to stir from a deep sleep. Mary coughed once, twice and then placed her hand on her throat.

Mary's eyes bulged and she began to cough up leeches.

Mary gasped, "Samuel, I cannot breathe."

Mary, unable to clear all the leeches from her mouth and throat, began to gag.

Doctor Edwards woke with a start and fumbled in the darkness.

Doctor Edwards said, "Light the lamp. Where are you, Mary?"

Mary's body shook and she began to turn blue.

Mary tried to say, "Help me," but she could no longer speak, could no longer breathe.

Doctor Edwards rubbed his eyes and then he screamed. "There are leeches on my eyes!"

In the darkness, Doctor Edwards stumbled out of bed and slowly, blindly, felt his way towards the stairs.

Doctor Edwards tripped over a chair as he approached the stairs.

Again, the doctor started to scream. "Someone, please! I need help! I cannot see! I cannot find the stairs!"

Doctor Edwards got to his feet slowly, feeling his way in the darkness.

Doctor Edwards put both hands on the wall and moved towards the stairs very slowly, using the wall as a guide.

As he crept, slowly, through the dark house, Doctor Edwards was taken by surprise when his right foot suddenly fell, with a heavy thud, onto the stairs he had been trying to locate.

As he tried to maintain his balance, Doctor Edwards fell, quickly and violently, down the stairs.

When he reached the bottom of the stairs, Doctor Edwards' head hit the floor with a sickening crack and his neck broke.

The house was quiet.

• • •*

Grandmother Rose said, "Marcus, were you able to obtain the item I requested?"

Marcus smiled and handed Grandmother Rose a small burlap sack.

Grandmother Rose reached into the sack and pulled out Nancy Kelley's doll.

Carefully, Grandmother Rose placed the doll into the cauldron.

The doll floated on top of the boiling witches' brew.

• • •

Nancy Kelley, now an unrecognizable mass of hideous lesions, lay in her bed, fighting for every breath.

• • •

Grandmother Rose lightly touched Nancy's doll as it floated in the cauldron. "Let no harm come to this child by gallows, fire or pox."

The doll's face and body began to break out in horrifying smallpox lesions.

• • •

The lesions disappeared from Nancy Kelley's face and body.

Nancy Kelley, now the picture of health, jumped out of bed and rushed into her parents' arms.

June and Harrison Kelley embraced their daughter and fought back tears.

• • •

As the morning sun began to illuminate Grandmother Rose's herb garden, Nancy Kelley's horribly disfigured doll slowly sank to the bottom of the cauldron.

Grandmother Rose wiped sweat from her forehead.

Marcus poured water on the fire and stirred the smoking ashes with a stick.

Grandmother Rose said, "I think we will have breakfast here in the herb garden this morning, Marcus."

"That sounds lovely," said Widow Wheeler.

"It does," agreed Mrs. Black.

Marcus said, "Tea and porridge and eggs and meat, Grandmother Rose. It will be ready for you very soon."

Grandmother Rose said, "Yes, please. As soon as you can, Marcus. It has been a long night. We are all famished."

55.

LEAVES CHANGED COLOR AND DIED, Salem was buried under snow, icicles slowly melted, spring thawed the colony, and Lilly's memory began to return. The old woman was Grandmother Rose, Lilly was sure of it. Lilly had lived with Grandmother Rose once, had been happy in her home. But then, but then…it was hard to remember exactly, everything was still shrouded in a heavy mist. Lilly had to block everything out, had to concentrate, and when she did, she saw a handsome young man named Kyle Edwards. She had loved him passionately. She had trusted him. Lilly knew something had happened. Something terrible. There was fire. And her friend, Susan. Burning. Screaming. Terrible men. Magistrates. Lilly remembered certain names and faces and events but the memories were still not entirely clear.

However, despite her befogged memory, Lilly knew, with great certainty, that Grandmother Rose was a witch! And Lilly knew that she, too was a witch. That was why she had survived the fire that destroyed Susan. Grandmother Rose had given her that information in a terrible place, a dungeon or a gaol cell. Grandmother Rosc had taught her that fire could not kill a witch.

And Grandmother Rose had been right, because, despite the flames, Lilly still had form. True, she did not have a real, solid, human body, she was still airy and light, she was still transparent and ethereal, but she was starting to look a little bit more human with each passing day.

And she was, now, more attached to Salem. She no longer had the desire to fly through heavy clouds or to dance on raindrops. Nor did she wish to hover over rough, roiling oceans or to soar, rapidly, above craggy mountain tops and majestic eagles. No, now all Lilly wanted was to be in Salem. Where she had once had a life.

Instead of roaming the skies, Lilly now enjoyed visiting all the places she had loved when she had been alive. In her present circumstances, she thought of them as her old haunts. (And that thought had amused her enormously.)

She had slowly drifted through Grandmother Rose's herb garden and the hayloft she had enjoyed with Kyle. She had hung in the air, suspended above the gristmill's huge, overshot water wheel. She had even drifted into Bay Church. (During a service!) None of the parishioners had noticed her. She had watched Reverend Simpson's service from high above, just below the roof while resting on one of the wooden rafters where the rats loved to scurry. The rats had not bothered her. They had sensed her presence, her energy, and they had kept their distance. And she had watched the service and listened to the words and the music and she had smiled.

Lilly missed being alive.

56.

KYLE EDWARDS, SHIRTLESS, chopped firewood under the hot midday sun.

A very pregnant Catherine sat under the shade of a Weeping Willow tree, sipping lemonade and watching Kyle. "It is unusually hot for spring, Kyle. Please, rest a while. Have a drink with me."

Kyle continued to chop wood. "I am perfectly fine, Catherine. You are the one who needs to rest. Go inside and sleep a while. You will need your strength very soon."

"No, I prefer to stay out here. The house is far too hot. And in any event, I am not tired and the baby is still weeks away. Let us speak of something else."

• • •

Grandmother Rose sat in her herb garden sipping tea as Marcus applied white paint to a wooden baby's cradle.

Grandmother Rose squeezed lemon into her tea and said, "I need it for tonight, Marcus. The baby is coming tonight."

Marcus wiped sweat from his brow. "It will be finished."

Grandmother Rose looked heavenward. The hot sun momentarily blinded her and she shielded her eyes with one hand. "There is a storm coming. The weather change will bring the baby."

Marcus smiled. "So much easier when you know what is coming."

Grandmother Rose said, "Unfortunately, Marcus, what will happen tonight will not be easy."

• • •

As Kyle continued to chop wood, dark clouds rolled in, blocking the sun.

A strong wind knocked over Catherine's glass of lemonade. "Oh! Kyle, it was so beautiful just a moment ago."

Long branches of lightning streaked across the sky and then thunder exploded over Salem.

Rain dropped down, suddenly, in sheets.

Kyle put down his axe and hurried toward Catherine.

Kyle picked Catherine up and carried her into the house, up the stairs and into the bedroom.

Kyle kissed Catherine and then carefully placed her on the bed.

Catherine said, "I love you, Kyle. I -"

Catherine grabbed her abdomen and winced in pain.

Concerned, Kyle asked, "What is it, Catherine? What is wrong?"

Catherine breathed deeply and then smiled. "It is nothing. Just a momentary pain. Could you bring me some water, please?"

Kyle quickly left the bedroom.

As soon as Kyle was gone, Catherine shut her eyes, rubbed her abdomen and began to moan.

Kyle returned with the water.

Again, Catherine smiled in an attempt to hide her pain.

Kyle handed Catherine the glass of water and she sipped it, slowly.

Catherine grabbed her abdomen again. The glass of water fell to the wooden floor and shattered. "My God, Kyle! The baby is coming. Help me!"

Kyle, terrified, said, "If only my father were alive. We need a doctor."

Catherine wiped sweat from her forehead. "There is no doctor now in Salem. You will have to do it all, Kyle."

Catherine grabbed her abdomen and screamed.

Kyle gathered Catherine up into his arms and carried her out into the storm.

Catherine screamed, "Kyle! Put me in our bed!"

Kyle shouted over the terrible noise of the storm. "Catherine, you need help! There is only one person…"

Kyle carried Catherine as quickly as he could, through the storm, through the streets of Salem.

57.

GRANDMOTHER ROSE, MRS. BLACK and Widow Wheeler sat quietly at Grandmother Rose's dining room table stitching a quilt as Marcus poured them tea and served them cake.

A sudden pounding on the front door shattered the peaceful moment and the women stopped working on their quilt and pushed aside their tea cups.

Marcus moved toward the door and said, "Who would be out in such a storm?"

Grandmother Rose said. "Leave it, Marcus. I will answer the door. It is for me."

Grandmother Rose calmly walked to the front door and then opened it.

Kyle, soaking wet, stood on the doorstep holding Catherine in his arms.

Kyle pleaded, "I know you hate me but please, for the sake of this baby. I have heard people talk. They say you have guided many of Salem's women through childbirth. You must help."

Grandmother Rose said, "Come in, Kyle."

Kyle carried Catherine into the house.

Grandmother Rose said, "Marcus, carry Catherine upstairs. Put her on my bed. I will be right there."

Kyle carefully placed Catherine in Marcus's arms and then Marcus carried Catherine up the stairs.

Kyle said to Grandmother Rose, "Thank you."

Grandmother Rose looked at Kyle. "You are shivering Kyle. Go and stand by the fire."

Grandmother Rose lifted a bottle of whiskey from a sideboard in the dining room and then handed the bottle to Kyle.

Grandmother Rose said, "Drink some of this, Kyle. It will be a long night."

Grandmother Rose, Mrs. Black and Widow Wheeler walked up the stairs, leaving Kyle alone in the dining room.

As she climbed the stairs, Grandmother Rose looked down at Kyle and said, "When I see you next, you will have a child."

Kyle smiled and drank some of the whiskey, straight from the bottle.

58.

CATHERINE LAY, NAKED, on Grandmother Rose's canopy bed, her body covered by a white sheet.

Mrs. Black held Catherine's right hand.

Widow Wheeler held Catherine's left hand.

Grandmother Rose rubbed a clear fluid onto Catherine's abdomen.

Catherine's forehead was beaded with sweat. She said to Grandmother Rose, "The pain is going away."

Grandmother Rose continued to rub the clear fluid onto Catherine's abdomen. "Just shut your eyes and breathe deeply."

Catherine said, "I feel a strange pressure."

A red stain began to spread across the lower half of the white sheet.

Grandmother Rose removed the sheet and examined Catherine. "There is a problem, ladies. She is too small. The baby is tearing her. We must stop the bleeding."

Mrs. Black took a crystal goblet filled with thick brown liquid from Grandmother Rose's nightstand and pressed it to Catherine's lips. "You are hemorrhaging, child. Drink this down. It will stop your bleeding."

Catherine tasted the liquid and then pushed the goblet away. "I will not drink it. It is too horrible."

Mrs. Black said, "Yes, I know it is truly foul but you must drink it."

Again, Mrs. Black pressed the goblet to Catherine's lips.

Catherine winced, grabbed the goblet and threw it against the bedroom wall.

The goblet shattered.

Mrs. Black said, "Stupid girl."

Grandmother Rose said to Mrs. Black, "There is no time for that now, the baby is coming. Get Marcus!"

Mrs. Black hurried from the bedroom.

Grandmother Rose said to Catherine, "Just another minute now. Try to be calm."

Catherine screamed as Marcus and Mrs. Black rushed into the bedroom.

Grandmother Rose said, "The head is coming out. Hold it firmly, Marcus."

Marcus did as Grandmother Rose instructed and then he said, "I have it. I have the baby. It is a girl."

Marcus held up the bloody, screaming infant for all to see.

Grandmother Rose shut her eyes and said, "Now, Lilly."

Lilly's spectral form suddenly appeared in the bedroom and stood next to Marcus. Lilly's ghost was fully-formed, almost solid, almost human in appearance.

Catherine's eyes widened in terror. "Lilly Parris! It is not possible. I saw you burned!"

Lilly looked at Catherine and smiled.

Widow Wheeler laughed softly. "Stupid girl. You cannot burn a witch."

Terrified, Catherine shouted, "Oh, God. Save me from these witches!"

Grandmother Rose ignored Catherine and yelled, "Do it, Lilly! Do it now!"

Lilly's ghost lifted off the ground, turned to mist and entered the mouth of the screaming infant who inhaled the mist, gasped, and then stopped screaming.

Grandmother Rose smiled and then said to the infant, "Welcome back, Lilly."

59.

FIERCE SPRING RAIN, roaring thunder and hot white lightning continued to terrorize Salem but Kyle, now comfortably drunk and oblivious to the storm, sat at the dining room table and sipped whiskey as Grandmother Rose, Mrs. Black, Widow Wheeler and Marcus walked back into the room.

Marcus held baby Lilly who had been washed and wrapped in a blanket.

Grandmother Rose said, "You have a daughter, Kyle."

Kyle, slightly wobbly on his feet, carefully took the baby from Marcus and kissed it on the forehead.

Kyle looked at the baby for a moment and then said, "She is so beautiful. Just like her mother. Do you not agree?"

Grandmother Rose did not respond.

Kyle asked, "Is Catherine awake? Does she have much pain?"

Grandmother Rose said, "She is gone."

Marcus took baby Lilly from Kyle.

Kyle asked, angrily, "What are you saying, old woman? You killed Catherine? You killed my wife?"

DANIEL SUGAR

Grandmother Rose spoke slowly and calmly. "There was simply too much blood loss. No one is to blame. These things sometimes happen during childbirth."

Kyle lunged at Grandmother Rose and knocked her to the floor. "Incompetent hag! I will kill you! I will smash your skull!"

Kyle grabbed the whiskey bottle from the dining room table and raised it up into the air.

Grandmother Rose's eyes narrowed and she held up one hand and calmly said, "Stop."

Kyle stopped dead. He dropped the whiskey bottle and it fell to the floor and shattered. "Old woman, I will kill you, I will - "

Kyle put his hands on his chest and then doubled over in pain.

Mrs. Black and Widow Wheeler helped Grandmother Rose to her feet.

Marcus, still holding baby Lilly, walked towards Kyle.

Kyle moaned and then collapsed onto the dining room floor. "I cannot breathe. My chest."

Kyle looked at the baby, Marcus, Grandmother Rose, Widow Wheeler and Mrs. Black and realized they were all fading away. Everything was fading away.

60.

IN THE MORNING, the long, terrible thunderstorm was nothing but a memory and cool, bright spring sunshine illuminated the Bay Church Cemetery funeral service for Kyle and Catherine Edwards, (which was brief and poorly- attended). Only Reverend Simpson, Grandmother Rose, Mrs. Black, Widow Wheeler and two gravediggers remained at the gravesite after the final prayers were spoken.

Grandmother Rose, Mrs. Black and Widow Wheeler tossed roses onto the caskets and Reverend Simpson bowed his head as the gravediggers lowered the caskets into the ground.

Grandmother Rose said, "A tragedy, ladies."

Mrs. Black and Widow Wheeler nodded their heads in agreement.

The gravediggers began to shovel dirt into the graves.

Reverend Simpson said, "The strain of his wife's sudden death was just too much for his heart, poor boy."

Mrs. Black said, "It is as if he is still here. It is as if he has not really left us."

Widow Wheeler said, "I feel that too, Mrs. Black. I still feel his presence."

Reverend Simpson said, "The shock of a young death is what you feel, my good women. It is not an uncommon phenomenon. It is perfectly normal for the living to believe that the dear departed is still alive."

Grandmother Rose said, "You are so wise, Reverend Simpson. So very wise."

Reverend Simpson smiled at the flattering words and lightly touched Grandmother Rose's arm. "It is my job to know these things, Grandmother Rose. I am simply doing my job."

61.

ONE HOUR AFTER LEAVING the graveyard, Grandmother Rose welcomed Peter Andrews as he walked into her sunny herb garden. "Mister Andrews, I am so glad you were able to accept my invitation to a farewell breakfast."

"Thank you for your kindness."

Grandmother Rose pointed to a table that Marcus was busily topping with biscuits, fruit preserves, hard boiled eggs, roast chicken, wine and beer. "Marcus has prepared a feast for us. I do hope you are hungry."

Peter Andrews smiled and nodded and then he took a long look around the herb garden. "Forgive me, Grandmother Rose, I hope I do not seem rude or distracted, it is just that this is truly the most extraordinary garden. I do not believe I have ever seen so many herbs."

"I am quite proud of it, Mister Andrews. I have quite a variety growing here."

Grandmother Rose poured two cups of tea, handed one to Peter Andrews and then picked up the other cup, took a sip and walked over to an herb that had a spotted stem and white flowers.

Grandmother Rose lightly touched the white flowers. "This is hemlock, Mister Andrews. A powerful sedative. This little devil can cause symptoms that mimic a heart attack. If someone put enough of this in your food or drink you could actually be taken for dead. Fortunately, it always wears off. Eventually."

Grandmother Rose sat down at the table and continued to sip her tea.

Peter Andrews watched Grandmother Rose intently as she drank her tea and he thought he detected an almost imperceptible smile playing at the corners of her lips.

• • •

As Grandmother Rose and Peter Andrews sat in the herb garden and ate the delicious breakfast Marcus had prepared, Kyle Edwards, lying in his coffin, suddenly woke up.

As Kyle's eyes slowly adjusted to the darkness, he was able to make out the dark wood that surrounded him.

Kyle pounded on the wood that covered him and began to scream. "Can you hear me? Are you out there? I am not dead! The old bitch has tricked you! She has my baby! I am not dead!"

• • •

Six feet above Kyle's coffin, children, (oblivious to Kyle Edwards' terrified screams), ran through Bay Church Cemetery, playing, laughing, shouting.

• • •

Peter Andrews helped himself to a large, juicy, slice of roast chicken and then said, "I believe you are an extremely interesting woman, Grandmother Rose."

Grandmother Rose smiled. "Mister Andrews, I believe you are correct."

Peter Andrews quickly washed the chicken down with a mug of beer and then shook Grandmother Rose's hand. "Thank you for a most delicious breakfast."

"You are always welcome in this garden and in my home. I hope you will be a frequent visitor, despite the great distance between Salem and Boston."

Peter Andrews stood up and addressed Marcus. "Speaking of Boston, the horses are ready. Are you set, Marcus?"

Marcus said, "Yes, I am ready. But I just cannot believe I will be riding into Boston a free man."

Grandmother Rose said, "Marcus, you will be magnificent. A fine, upstanding addition to Boston."

Marcus embraced Grandmother Rose.

Grandmother Rose pressed Lilly's crucifix into Marcus's right hand. "Wear it always. Promise me."

Marcus had not cried since he was a small child but he could feel the tears coming. He could barely look at Grandmother Rose as he said, "I promise. But if I do not leave now I will never be able to go."

Grandmother Rose quickly said, "I understand. You go now. I will say your goodbyes to Mrs. Black and Widow Wheeler."

Without looking back, Marcus quickly left the herb garden.

Peter Andrews smiled at Grandmother Rose and then followed Marcus.

Grandmother Rose sighed and then walked into the house and climbed the stairs to her bedroom where she discovered a fire burning in the fireplace and Mrs. Black and Widow Wheeler sitting on the bed.

Alice Mead, a pretty, African American teenager, sat in a rocking chair next to the fireplace and gently rocked baby Lilly.

Grandmother Rose laughed. "Well, this is a pretty picture."

Alice said, "She is such a good baby. She has not cried once. Would you like to rock her, Ma'am?"

Grandmother Rose smiled. "When she is older, Alice. When she is older."

Alice nodded and continued to rock baby Lilly.

Grandmother Rose clapped her hands and said to her friends, "Up off the bed with you. We have an appointment to keep in the herb garden. Have you both forgotten? We have company coming for tea."

62.

ALICE SERVED TEA AND CAKES to Grandmother Rose, Mrs. Black, Widow Wheeler and Tom Marks.

Tom nibbled on his cake and said, "It was kind of you to invite me, this morning, Rose. I did not expect it."

Grandmother Rose put down her teacup and said, "I hold no grudge, Tom. What happened was for the best. We all know the stain on my family name had to be erased. Still, I have been feeling lonely so it was kind of you to visit."

"You are an enlightened woman, Rose. For the good of Salem itself, we must put this unpleasant situation behind us."

Grandmother Rose smiled sweetly. "I could not agree more, Tom. And that is why I have decided to fill in the foundation this very day."

Tom Marks said, "Foundation?"

Grandmother Rose refilled Tom's teacup. "I was planning a honeymoon cottage for the young couple just beyond my apple orchard. The foundation was in its very early stages. Nothing more than a deep pit, really. But I am strong and I can still lift a shovel, so I am going to take care of the matter today."

Tom drained his teacup. "Nonsense. I will not let you shovel one ounce of earth. I will take care of everything."

Mrs. Black took a bite of her cake and said, "Such a gentleman."

Widow Wheeler squeezed lemon juice into her tea and said, "Indeed."

63.

TOM MARKS, GRANDMOTHER Rose, Mrs. Black and Widow Wheeler walked through the sunny apple orchard carrying shovels.

Tom Marks said to Grandmother Rose, "I must say, Rose, if you were planning to build, you certainly kept it a secret. Where is this so-called foundation?"

Grandmother Rose laughed. "I will admit, Tom, if one did not know where to look, well, let us just say it is not easily found."

Mrs. Black pointed straight ahead. "There. Just yards from here."

The foursome walked on and then came to a stop at the edge of a deep pit.

Tom Marks looked down into the pit. "This is the foundation? It is really more of a well. It must be eight feet deep."

Widow Wheeler said, "Closer to twelve. Anyone that falls in does not get out."

Tom nodded in agreement. "I should think not. Although the fall alone would probably be fatal."

Grandmother Rose said, "Let us test that theory, ladies."

Grandmother Rose, Mrs. Black and Widow Wheeler joined hands and began to hum.

Tom Marks looked at the three women and said, angrily, "What is this? Have you all suddenly gone mad?"

The three witches shut their eyes and then Tom Marks slowly began to rise up into the air.

Tom Marks screamed, "What evil is this? Put me back to earth!" Tom waved his arms wildly and dropped his shovel.

The slave merchant, wandering through the apple orchard, stumbled upon the scene and watched, transfixed, from behind an apple tree. As he observed, the slave merchant whispered, "Witches, all three."

Again, Tom Marks screamed, "Put me back to earth!"

Grandmother Rose said, "Let us grant Tom's wish. Put him back to earth, ladies."

Tom Marks slowly moved through the air until he was directly over the deep pit.

Tom looked down at the pit and yelled, "No, please. Not that. Put me down!"

Grandmother Rose smiled. "Oh, we will put you down, Tom. We will put you down, forever."

The three witches stopped humming and opened their eyes.

Tom Marks dropped down into the deep pit and began to scream.

Grandmother Rose said, "Tom was mistaken. The fall is not enough to kill a person."

Mrs. Black said, "His screams are frightful. He must be terribly hurt."

Widow Wheeler raised her shovel. "Let us put him out of his misery."

Widow Wheeler shoveled dirt into the pit.

Tom Marks continued to scream.

Grandmother Rose touched Widow Wheeler's arm and said, "Slowly. Slowly."

As the three witches slowly filled the deep pit with dirt and Tom Marks' screams became more and more muffled, the slave merchant, still unseen, carefully, quietly, left his hiding place, made his way through the apple orchard and then returned to the center of Salem.

64.

THAT NIGHT in the herb garden, under the light of a bright spring moon, Grandmother Rose, Mrs. Black and Widow Wheeler sat at a table and sipped tea while Alice stood a few feet from the table and rocked a sleeping baby Lilly.

Grandmother Rose suddenly sensed something. She stood up and said, "Quickly, ladies. I have had a premonition. There is no time to lose.

"Alice, wrap the baby in blankets.

"Widow Wheeler, Mrs. Black, gather up only what you absolutely need.

"We must get to the port, ladies. Immediately."

Confused, Alice said, "I do not understand, Ma'am. I -"

Grandmother Rose shouted. "Do as I say!"

Alice, Widow Wheeler and Mrs. Black rushed off to do Grandmother Rose's bidding.

Alone now in the herb garden, Grandmother Rose shut her eyes and said, "Hear me, Marcus. Touch the crucifix and hear me."

• • •

As Peter Andrews and Marcus rode through the forest, Marcus's crucifix began to glow. Marcus, oblivious, rubbed his neck and the crucifix slipped from its chain and fell to the ground.

• • •

Still standing alone in the herb garden with her eyes shut, Grandmother Rose said, "I need you, Marcus. Come quickly."

• • •

Peter and Marcus continued to ride through the dark forest, away from Salem.

The crucifix, still glowing, lay on the forest floor.

65.

AN ARMED MOB ON HORSEBACK, led by the slave merchant, made its way through the streets of Salem.

The slave merchant raised his musket in the air and yelled, "Follow me now, all of you! We will rid Salem of all its witches!"

The crowd screamed its approval.

A young man lifted a torch high in the air and shouted, "Kill the old women! Kill the old witches!"

Again, the crowd cheered.

The slave merchant viciously whipped his horse and then quickly rode away.

The mob followed.

• • •

Alice rushed into Grandmother Rose's bedroom and carefully placed baby Lilly in a wicker basket.

As Alice was about to pick up the wicker basket, a torch crashed through the bedroom window and caught the hem of Alice's floor-length cotton dress.

Alice screamed as her dress ignited and she was engulfed in flames.

Mrs. Black grabbed the wicker basket just as the slave merchant climbed through the broken window.

Mrs. Black looked back at the bedroom as she rushed toward the stairs and saw the slave merchant aim his musket at Alice.

The slave merchant said, "Die twice, witch. Once by fire, once by bullet."

The slave merchant shot Alice and she fell, dead, to the floor.

• • •

Mrs. Black, Widow Wheeler and Grandmother Rose, carrying the wicker basket that held baby Lilly, rushed from the house, quickly mounted horses and rode off into the night.

• • •

The slave merchant looked out the broken bedroom window and desperately scanned the grounds surrounding the house. The three witches were barely visible as they rode away under cover of darkness.

The slave merchant rushed outside and mounted his horse just as the armed mob on horseback finally caught up to him and arrived at Grandmother Rose's house.

The slave merchant addressed the mob. "I believe the witches will now head to the port. We can still intercept them at Gallows Hill if we hurry. All of you, follow me!"

The slave merchant whipped his horse and rode off toward Gallows Hills.

• • •

The slave merchant led the mob to the base of Gallows Hill just as Grandmother Rose, Mrs. Black and Widow Wheeler rode across the top of the hill.

The slave merchant pointed and screamed, "There! At the top of the hill. We have them. Quickly now, all of you, surround the hill. The witches are trapped!"

The mob quickly surrounded Gallows Hill.

• • •

Grandmother Rose saw that Gallows Hill was surrounded. There was no escape.

Grandmother Rose quickly pulled back on her horse's reins.

The horse stopped and Grandmother Rose, still carrying the wicker basket, dismounted.

Mrs. Black and Widow Wheeler also dismounted.

Grandmother Rose said, "We must be strong now, witches. For Lilly's sake, we must find a way to survive."

The slave merchant and the mob approached the three women.

The slave merchant said to Grandmother Rose, "Give me the basket, old woman. I promise the baby will not be harmed. Give me the child."

Defiantly, Grandmother Rose said, "You will not touch this child. Not while I am alive."

The slave merchant laughed. "Trust me, old witch, your time on this earth has run its course."

Two young men screamed, broke free from the mob and rushed towards Mrs. Black and Widow Wheeler. The men quickly slipped nooses over the women's necks and then dragged them to the scaffold.

The mob erupted, shouting and cheering as the young men hanged Mrs. Black and Widow Wheeler.

Grandmother Rose watched her friends die and said, "Evil, foolish Salemites."

Again, the slave merchant addressed Grandmother Rose. "Put the child down, old woman. You die now."

The slave merchant took a noose from his jacket pocket and calmly walked toward Grandmother Rose.

The slave merchant grabbed Grandmother Rose and began to lower the noose over her head.

Grandmother Rose shut her eyes and put the wicker basket on the ground.

A shot rang out.

The slave merchant dropped the noose and grabbed his bleeding arm.

Peter Andrews rode past the slave merchant and scooped up the wicker basket.

Marcus grabbed Grandmother Rose, pulled her onto his horse and galloped through the stunned mob of Salemites.

The slave merchant screamed at the mob. "You fools! If they reach the port, all is lost!"

The slave merchant, covered in blood, mounted his horse and gave chase.

66.

Grandmother Rose, Marcus and Peter Andrews reached the port of Salem and then quickly dismounted.

As the trio ran along the dock toward the ships, the slave merchant galloped onto the dock, leapt off his horse and screamed, "I want the slave, Marcus Cooper! No weapons! Bare fists alone!"

Grandmother Rose said, "You must not do this, Marcus," as the mob following the slave merchant slowly made its way onto the dock.

Marcus replied, "There is nothing to fear. I do it for you, for Lilly, for Susan."

The mob fell silent as Marcus took off his shirt and then faced the slave merchant.

Peter touched Marcus's arm and said, "Be very careful, Marcus. He is not to be trusted."

The slave merchant lunged and punched Marcus in the face.

Marcus, stunned, fell onto the dock.

The slave merchant laughed and said, "This is giving me great joy."

The slave merchant kicked Marcus in the face, knocking out several of Marcus's teeth.

Grandmother Rose said, "Get up, Marcus."

The slave merchant spat at Grandmother Rose. "Shut up, old woman!"

The slave merchant kicked Marcus in the stomach.

Marcus wheezed and coughed up blood.

Marcus looked at the slave merchant. The man was a blur.

Grandmother Rose said, "Be strong, Marcus."

Marcus's vision began to clear and he slowly stood up.

The slave merchant laughed.

Marcus lunged, knocked the slave merchant to the ground, jumped on top of him and then pinned the slave merchant's arms to the ground.

The slave merchant struggled but could not move.

Marcus said, "Now, you will call off your mob and ensure our safety until we are well out of Salem. Do this and I will spare your miserable life."

The slave merchant said nothing and continued to struggle.

Marcus put his hands around the slave merchant's throat and began to squeeze. "Do this or die!"

The slave merchant managed to gasp, "Very well. You have my word. We will let you go."

Slowly, Marcus eased his grip on the slave merchant's throat.

Marcus got to his feet and turned toward Grandmother Rose and Peter Andrews.

Grandmother Rose shouted, "Take care, Marcus!"

As Marcus turned toward Grandmother Rose and Peter Andrews, the slave merchant pulled a small knife from his boot, sprang to his feet and plunged the knife into Marcus's back.

Marcus gasped, doubled over and then collapsed onto the dock.

Peter Andrews yelled, "No!"

Peter put down the wicker basket, grabbed the slave merchant's head and twisted it violently, snapping the slave merchant's neck.

Peter, crying, knelt down, cradled Marcus in his arms and quietly said, "Marcus, don't leave me."

Marcus reached up and touched Peter's face. "There is nothing more to fear. Take Grandmother Rose and Lilly and go."

Marcus died and the mob of Salemites slowly moved toward Grandmother Rose and Peter Andrews.

Quickly, Grandmother Rose raised her arms and shut her eyes. Then, she began to hum.

A wall of fire sprang up and surrounded the mob. The mob was trapped, unable to move.

Grandmother Rose grabbed the wicker basket, took Peter Andrews' hand and together they ran along the dock and onto a ship.

As Peter Andrews safely sailed the ship away from the port of Salem, the wall of fire spread, first to all the other ships in the port and, then, to Main Street and Gallows Hill.

As the ship moved swiftly along the water, Grandmother Rose looked back at Salem. The fires that dotted the village blazed like lighthouse beacons, illuminating the night. "Burn, evil village. Live in infamy."

Peter Andrews said, "The fire will purify their souls, once and for all."

Grandmother Rose touched Peter Andrews' shoulder. "Look away now. Look ahead."

Grandmother Rose and Peter Andrews turned their backs on Salem and then Peter knelt down, reached into the wicker basket and gently stroked baby Lilly's head.

As the ship sailed forward, slicing through the warm night air, Lilly smiled.

EPILOGUE

TEN-YEAR-OLD LILLY PARRIS clutched her small bible and inhaled the crisp autumn air as she walked along Ile de la Cite in the fourth arrondissement. Oh, how she loved Paris! The architecture, the paintings, the food and, of course, the fashion.

Lilly ran her hand over her fine light blue silk dress trimmed with spotted gauze. Grandmother Rose had given it to her that very morning as a tenth birthday present. And Peter Andrews had presented her with a pair of dark purple silk shoes that were the most comfortable she had ever worn.

Lilly looked at Grandmother Rose and Peter Andrews as they walked beside her in the cool morning air. How fine they both looked, dressed in the latest French fashions. Peter was so very handsome in his knee-length, honey-colored justaucorps coat, white cravat, three-button white silk waistcoat, beige breeches and white stockings. And Grandmother Rose, so striking in a black calash bonnet, a black, thigh-length caraco jacket, a black, quilted, silk charmeuse skirt and a scarlet cashmere shawl.

Lilly almost shivered with delight as she thought about how lucky she was to live with Grandmother Rose and Peter Andrews. She truly was the most fortunate girl in the world. The big, beautiful hotel in which they all lived on the Faubourg Saint-Germain reminded her of a castle. It had wonderful long hallways she could run through and wide courtyards in which she and her friends could play - it even had a large herb garden that seemed to fascinate Grandmother Rose.

Yes, she was lucky. And even more so today because Grandmother Rose and Peter Andrews had finally agreed to take her to her favorite church, Notre Dame, for her birthday. Lilly loved churches and Notre Dame was the most magnificent church in Paris. Lilly had been to many wonderful churches in Paris but she had always longed to visit the greatest church of all: Notre Dame.

Suddenly Notre Dame's great spire came into view and Lilly's heart began to beat rapidly. She could already see the gargoyles and the stunning rose window. "Oh, Grandmother Rose, thank you for bringing me here. It is magnificent."

Grandmother Rose laughed. "Not many young girls ask to go to church on their birthday, but if this is what makes you happy…"

Lilly kept walking and had to force herself not to run - she was so eager to get inside and finally explore Notre Dame. "Oh, it is. It is. I could not ask for a better birthday present."

Peter Andrews smiled. "I think Paris agrees with you, Lilly."

Lilly said, "Oh, Peter, it truly does. I cannot think of a better place in all the world. Do you not love it as I do?"

"Lilly, I feel fortunate to live in a place of such enlightenment. Paris is a city of visionaries," Peter responded.

"It is true," said Grandmother Rose. "You can feel it as you stroll through Paris. The people are so advanced, so tolerant."

As the trio continued to walk toward Notre Dame, they passed an alleyway where four young men were working. Distracted, Grandmother Rose, Lilly and Peter Andrews did not notice the four men who used hammers to pound nails into a large wooden frame. When the men were satisfied the frame was secure, they placed a large, heavy, wedge-shaped blade into the frame. The men then lifted the blade to the top of the frame, positioned a crude, life-sized mannequin on the frame's base and then released the blade. The heavy blade fell rapidly and loudly and sliced off the mannequin's head. The men, pleased with the result, smiled and clasped each other's hands and offered loud congratulations.

As Grandmother Rose, Lilly and Peter Andrews walked into Notre Dame, Lilly gasped. The interior of the enormous, delicate, Gothic church seemed to glow; lit by the magnificent light of Paris.

It was unlike any church Lilly had ever seen and as she hungrily looked around, as she tried to absorb the magnificence, she thought of another church. And Lilly suddenly realized that every time she stepped into any church she thought of a much smaller, wooden church.

A church she knew with great certainty she had been in even though she could not remember its name or where it was. The memory was shrouded in mist. Occasionally, there would even be a flash of some of the people in that church: a very handsome young man, a pretty, dark-skinned young woman, an older, angry face screaming with rage; but she could never make the faces out completely, could never understand who they were or what they were trying to say to her. Nevertheless, it all seemed so real, as though all of those people were reaching out to her from another place, another time, trying to make their voices heard. Lilly hoped that eventually their faces and voices would become clear and she would finally understand exactly what it was they were all trying to tell her. She hoped that one day the veil of mist that fogged her memory would lift and she would finally solve the tantalizing puzzle, would finally recognize the people calling out to her and know the story of their lives.

There was no need to be impatient. There was no need to feel frustrated. Lilly had all the time in the world to put the intractable puzzle pieces together. And she would do it in Paris, the charming, friendly, peaceful city that she loved. She would live there forever. And nothing would ever go wrong…

LILLY WILL RETURN IN

THE WITCH AND
THE GUILLOTINE